THE EVACUEE

Kate Bolton

*With grateful thanks to my long suffering husband, Keith,
for all the computer help to get my book published.*

CONTENTS

CHAPTER 1

Mavis squeals, clutching at my hand as the train whooshes into the black cavern of the tunnel with a simultaneous blast of air and hooter, steam billowing past the windows and the smell of soot creeping through the window.

I pat my wife's hand reassuringly and she giggles at her fright.

'We must be coming into the station', I say, twenty intervening years suddenly disappearing from my memory, as the train slows to a hissing, cloud-ridden halt and whistles blow, guards shout, doors bang open, cases bump out onto the platform.

I heave our two cases down from the rack and follow Mavis onto the platform.

Ventnor.

'Well, here we are my love. Sunny Isle of Wight.'

And indeed it is a glorious day, unlike the cloud cover we left behind in Lewes.

'Shouldn't we queue for the taxi, Jack?' Mavis prompts me as I lead the way out of the station.

I'm afraid a selfish need to savour this moment takes over, and I cross the main road to look out and down over the wide panorama that is Ventnor and Bonchurch, hunkering low between the high Boniface downs to the north and the huge sparkling English Channel to the south, Azure blue under this cloudless June sky. What an absolutely perfect day to start a week's holi-

1

day and a trip down memory lane.

'Is it how you remember it?' Mavis tentatively intrudes on my thoughts and I remember my manners and link my arm through hers.

'It looks just the same, I think, only smaller'

Perhaps that's because we are way up here. I remember everything being really steep wherever we walked, so perhaps my sensible wife was right, we should have grabbed a taxi!

I look back at the station and fortunately there is one just returning so I wave at it frantically and it obligingly turns around to collect us.

The guesthouse is small, a little dated, smells of lavender polish. Busy patterned pink wallpaper shouts into the bedroom space, competing with a mustard yellow counterpane, but the bed is large and soft, which is all that really matters on this first anniversary of our wedding.

The window looks south and we can just see a glimpse of the sea between two buildings in front of us. It is sparkling and inviting. Mavis discards her pink suit jacket before she disappears into the wallpaper and I rid my neck of the hot and scratchy tie before we both flop on the bed and make plans for what is left of the afternoon.

An hour and a half later we find ourselves enjoying an early evening drink outside The Anchor right on the front, Mavis sipping a chilled Liebfraumilch, me with a cold lager, watching the holiday makers departing from the beach, weary children carrying their buckets and spades up the steep cascade path back to their hotels and guesthouses. The air is full of the noise of children shouting and laughing, seagulls crying as they swoop around hoping for scraps, the rhythmic pull and push of the tide as the waves race up the shingle.

Twenty years since I was here. I didn't know then how much my life would change.

CHAPTER 2

EVACUATION, JULY 1940.

Waterloo Station. Children's voices, high pitched, excited, mixed into a strengthening brew of crying girls, sniveling boys, frazzled teachers shouting orders to deaf ears, parents shouting louder. Cardboard boxes housing gas masks bumping against skinny thighs, scuffed brown suitcases snagging small legs.

I stand obediently in line with classmates clutching my small worn suitcase and the horrible box with the scary gas mask, and feel the ordered chaos pressing in on me. I'm penned in by teachers, helpers, parents, shoulder to shoulder with my class 1 peers. I feel overwhelmed by the unknown.

My mate Jimmy is chatty and boisterous and seems to be treating this as an adventure as if he is privy to the unknown but anxiety gnaws at my gut because the 'unknown' looms larger and more scary the longer I stand here, coupled with fears of putting my case down and forgetting it, or being left behind somewhere if I don't pay attention.

Mum left about half an hour ago, soon after we arrived at the station.

She and I travelled on two buses to get here, setting off from the estate after I had breakfast, bleary eyed and still full of sleep.

Mum told me yesterday while I was having my breakfast that I was being evacuated. Boys at school and the teachers have been talking about it all week and I pretended I knew about it too rather than show them my ignorance. I didn't think evacuation applied to me so I didn't really pay attention. Some of the school children left on an evacuation trip early in the term but I didn't go so I didn't think I was going this time. It only started to sink in when Mum pulled the small case down from the top of the wardrobe and filled it quickly with my summer sandals, spare pants, a spare vest, and a couple of changes of clothes. She found an old pencil case in my drawer and put in a toothbrush and toothpaste. After she went downstairs to make some sandwiches for me I slipped Oscar, my woolly rabbit, under the top jumper. I think she'd tell me not to be a baby and leave him behind if she knew.

Mum tells me I'm going to the countryside where it will be safe from bombs. We've been hearing bomber planes most days and when Mum puts the wireless on in the evening the newsman tells us about somewhere else that has been hit. The bombs haven't fallen on the estate yet though.

I don't know where this countryside is that we're all going to but it must be further than I thought because we are all getting on a very long train which suddenly hisses steam in huge puffs onto the platform. Smell of soot in the hot and fuggy air that's swirling around steaming wool jackets and damp school mackintoshes. I'd like to take mine off but I daren't put my case down or the stupid gas mask. It was drizzling this morning so I wore my Mac like so many others did but now we are doomed to sweat.

I suppose I will be staying somewhere like a holiday place with some of my classmates, which might be fun. I don't usually get a holiday.

I'm not sure why Mum isn't being evacuated too, but I expect she'll be glad to have me out the way for a while. She often says 'Make yourself scarce, Jack', which means go to my bedroom, or in the summer I might go to Jimmy's and sometimes we head down to the pond with his older brother and throw stones to make ripples or try to catch minnows in his net.

My bedroom's okay, though. I have toy soldiers and a couple of annuals to look at the pictures, but the best thing is my model farm. I play with it a lot, arranging the cows in the green painted field, balancing the horse so he looks over the hedge because the hedge props him up on his three legs. I have a turkey, nearly as big as the horse, that I place in the back yard with the chickens. I can push the tractor around the track to the milking shed or the barn or back to the yard depending on what job the farmer wants to do that day. I think I'd like to be a farmer when I grow up.

I'm used to amusing myself, especially when Mum starts on the drink. It's best to become invisible then before she picks an argument. I also 'make myself scarce' when her man friend comes round. Bert is his name. He's the second one although there might have been more before that -I can't remember. I hate it when the men come in case they talk to me in that jokey sort of way that adults do to children which isn't really funny but I have to laugh as if it is. I prefer to 'disappear' before Bert turns up.

After shuffling from foot to foot for an eternity, inching forward in our crocodile, teachers shouting above the noise, suggesting we go with Mrs Brooks to the toilet, to keep hold of our gas masks, to wave to parents, to listen and pay attention, we are divided up into smaller groups to fit into the carriages and I finally get to sit next to the window as the train pulls out with great billows of smoke blocking out the view. With clanking iron, squealing wheels, whistles and shouts, the train shunts forward with a sudden lurch. Mothers stand waving on the platform, some wiping their eyes with little handkerchiefs. I don't know why. It's not as if we're going anywhere for years. My mother has already left. She has things to do.

I fall asleep on the train and wake with a start leaning on Sheila Massy's shoulder which is a bit embarrassing. She pushes me up straight and says, 'you were snoring!'   That is even more embarrassing. I look out the window but I have no idea where we are, only that we are thundering through fields and hills on either side. This adventure is even more worrying now as we must be far from London and everyone's gone very quiet. One of the lady helpers is in our carriage but I don't know her name. She has her eyes closed.

I wonder if my Mum will miss me at all. I expect I'll be home again before she has much time to notice I'm not there. In the mornings she works in the Coop in the parade of shops down our road and when she's home she's always busy with something or other, cleaning and laundry mostly. Our yard is always strung with loads of clammy sheets that get in the way. They aren't all our sheets. Mum takes in other people's laundry too, although I don't know why they can't do it themselves. Mum says it brings in extra cash but that doesn't ever mean I can have an ice cream when we go to the shops. We only have a yard at the back, (Jimmy has a garden with a lawn and flower borders) There's a brick outhouse with the toilet, and the washing line is fixed from the toilet wall to next door's fence and back again in a zig zag.

I know we don't have much money because mum always mentions it if I want sweets or an ice cream.

'Money doesn't grow on trees, you know'.

Of course it doesn't, does she think I'm that stupid? It's not as if I ask for a bicycle or anything.

She gets in a real tizzy when I've grown out of my shoes as she says it costs 'an arm and a leg' for new ones. She often blames my Dad for us being poor, but I've never even seen my Dad. Mum says he 'went away' when I was born and then she uses a string of bad words for him so it's best not to ask anymore.

Pit's Wood Estate is huge. Our neighbour says it's the biggest council estate in England. I go to school at Pit's Wood Infant School which is right next door to the juniors. It takes about fifteen minutes to zig zag through the streets to the school. Mum took me there the first week until I knew the way and then I had to go by myself but generally I catch up with someone I know to walk with.

The train starts to slow down and our lady helper opens her eyes.

'We're coming into Portsmouth Harbour, children. Make sure you have your gas marks and all your other belongings. I'll fetch your cases down from the rack.'

I am now packed into a spacious hall in a place called the Winter Gardens. I haven't seen any gardens here, just a huge building with tall ceilings, and it's the middle of summer so it has a stupid name really. I feel awfully tired and would like to have a lie down.   I must be a long way from home as we've been travelling for hours and we even went on a boat which was a surprise. No one mentioned we were going on a boat. It was in a place called Portsmouth where the train stopped and we were all allowed out next to the harbour to eat our sandwiches. I could have guessed mine would be fish paste. I hate fish paste. I ate the bits in the middle and left all the crusts which I threw to the seagulls. They seemed to like fish paste better than I did so that made me feel better. I saw the sea for the first time in my whole five years. It was full of boats both huge and small. The tide was out and the harbour full of greenish mud with plenty of small rowing boats just sitting all lopsided waiting for the sea to wash back in and float them.

I must say, I did feel excited when we crowded onto the boat and it gave a great loud hoot as we left the dock, with puffs of black smoke belching from the funnel. It had a massive paddle on each side which made a whooshety whoosh sound through the waves. We sat on hard seats on the deck and we could look over the rails at the sea. It was a greeny brown colour with lots of choppy waves. I began to feel a tiny bit scared and I must have looked it because Miss Sands said, 'Are you alright Jack?' and I just nodded.

I found Jimmy and asked him if we were going to another country. He giggled and said, 'it's an Island, silly.'

How did he know all these things when I didn't?

Waves slapped against the sides and we dipped from side to side so we had trouble walking in a straight line until Miss Sands became agitated and told us all to sit down again.

After that, as if we hadn't been on enough transport, we all squashed into another train like the London Underground (that I've only been on once that I can remember) but this time we didn't go underground until the end.

Teachers and helpers took groups of children off the train at nearly every stop so there weren't many of us left when the train plunged suddenly into a black tunnel with a screeching whistle and we juddered to a halt at the station. The station had a strange word that was difficult for me to say. Ventnor.

Now I'm tired and fed up with this adventure and I miss my bedroom. I'm glad Jimmy is still in this group. He's the friend I like most although I do play with a few of the others sometimes.

Miss Sands and some of the other teachers organise us into lines where we queue at tables at the side of the room.

Some of the children are crying to go home. Some of us want the toilet, me included, and one of the teachers of the older children tuts at us and ushers us out into the foyer to find the gents. She's in a rush and bossily tells us to hurry up. It doesn't feel much like a holiday to me because no one seems to be in a happy holiday mood.

I'm one of the last to get back to the table I was queuing at and I look around for Jimmy who is disappearing out the door with a lady in a brown hat and brown suit.

There's another brown-suited lady hovering near me. The lady behind the table asks Miss Sands my name, although I could have told her myself. She reads the crumpled label on my Mackintosh which also has my name and she looks through her pile of papers. She peers over her spectacles at me and then back at Miss Sands.

'How old is he?'

She sounds puzzled.

'Five,' says Miss Sands, although I could have told her that as well. I'm actually nearly six, but no one seems to mention that.

'Hmm. It says fifteen here. Typing mistake I suppose.'

The woman makes a note on her papers and pulls out a card which she hands to the woman in the brown suit.

'Mrs Dyer at Warren Farm,' she says, and she and the brown lady exchange a strange look between them.

'Come on Jack, we're going to find your new home.'

Mrs Brown Suit ushers me out of the hall.

This time there is a blue and very rusty van outside in the car park and two older boys are waiting by the van talking to the driver who is leaning against the bonnet smoking a cigarette.

'Alright Mr Langdon we can go now. This one's for Warren Farm.'

The brown lady climbs into the van with the three of us and we chug up a steep hill into the town. I see a few straggling children with brown suit ladies walking up the hill and feel sort of special as we drive past in a motor vehicle.

We seem to climb up and up all the time with the old engine straining, finally turning right into a lane and then bumping along a cart track to a farm.

'We're here, Jack.' Mrs Brown Suit turns to me on the back seat. 'I'll come and introduce you to Mrs Dyer.'

The older boys stay in the van while I follow Mrs Brown Suit to the door of the farm house.

It feels so high here, we must be nearly touching the clouds. Green fields and hills all round and I can even see the misty blue sea in the distance. So far from anything I know and I suddenly feel close to tears. I wish even the older boys who I don't really know were staying here too, but now I feel so lonely I can't speak. I'm scared.

A lady, older than my Mum, comes to the door. Tall, wearing trousers, an old shirt and an apron. Her hair brown, wavy and untidy, falling onto her collar.

'Mrs Dyer? This is Jack Patton, your evacuee.'

Mrs Dyer looks down at me clutching my case and gas mask and then back at Mrs Brown Suit.

'He's young,' she says. 'I thought I was getting someone older.'

'There was a mistake on the papers with this one's age but a lot of people want older children, Mrs Dyer, and there's more younger ones to find homes for.'

Mrs Dyer gives a huge sigh, as if I'm a parcel that's been wrongly addressed and now she has to deal with it.

'You'd better come in then', she says, stepping back from the door as Mrs Brown Suit pats me on the back telling me she'll be calling round all the children in the week to see how they are settling in.

With that, the door is shut and I follow Mrs Dyer out of the spacious flagstone hallway into a vast kitchen that our whole house could fit into.

She looks me up and down with her hands on her hips as I stand there clutching my case and gas mask, wondering what I should do.

'Drink of milk?' she says.

I nod, then remember my manners and mumble, 'yes please.'

I'm glad she's asked because I'm really thirsty.

I dare to put my case down and take off the awful gas mask and hang it on the kitchen chair, one of eight arranged around a massive wooden table strewn with papers at one end, a basket of potatoes plonked in the middle along with a salt and pepper pot and a bowl of sugar.

Mrs Dyer brings me a large glass of milk, telling me to sit down, and fetches a plate with half a fruit cake on it.

She cuts me a wedge large enough to feed a family and sits down opposite.

We never have cake at home unless it's someone's birthday or Christmas, and I'd never be allowed a slice as generous as this. I remember my manners again and say thank you before tucking in. I didn't realise I was so hungry.

'What's your name again?'

'Jack', I mumble, trying not to spit cake crumbs.

'Well, Jack, I don't suppose you know much about farms.'

I want to mention that actually I do know a little about farms but I keep quiet. Anyway, my mouth is stuffed full of cake.

'You'll have to amuse yourself a lot here because I'm running this show on my own now, which is a lot of work. I was hoping to get another pair of hands to help me out, but I've got you instead'.

She shrugged her shoulders.

'Still, that's the way it is.'

She stands abruptly, wiping her hands down the front of her apron.

I'll show you your room and where everything is.'

She takes my case and I follow her up the stairs which lead out of the hallway and up into a landing with bannisters on one side looking down into the hall below.

My bedroom is about twice as big as the one at home with a very high double bed, dark wood headboard with carved flowers in the centre and the mattress topped with a dark green eiderdown. Everything seems very dark and there is a small window on one wall that looks down on a yard and across several stone buildings to fields beyond. I can see light brown cows in a sloping field to the right of a track. Outside one of the barns there is an old red tractor and I hope I can have a ride on it while I'm here.

'I hope you don't wet the bed,' says Mrs Dyer, looking sternly at me.

I shake my head, hoping that awful thing doesn't happen. It's been quite a while now since my sheets were wet.

'Come down to the kitchen when you've unpacked and I'll show you where you can collect the eggs. That can be your job.'

The bed is so high I have to clamber up to it and I sit cross legged on the green puffy pillows of the eiderdown, with dark bat's wings of trepidation flapping around my head, drawing tears of self pity and confusion.

I should be excited to be here on a farm where I can learn to be a farmer but I'm scared to be here on my own with Mrs Dyer who hasn't smiled yet and clearly doesn't want me here.

My mum always tells me what to do and right now she would take charge of unpacking my case and showing me where to put things. I hope Mrs Dyer shows me where the toilet is soon so I don't have to ask her.

I realise I'm still wearing my raincoat. No wonder I'm hot and I wrestle myself out of it, struggling with the buttons.

I slide off the bed and tackle the case. The catches are stiff and I need fingers of both hands to make them unlock. I look despondently into the case and instead of unpacking I just take out Oscar from under my second-best jumper and cuddle him tight, whispering my fears into one of his droopy ears and drying my wet cheeks on his woolly ones.

Emboldened by Oscar's therapy I venture downstairs and wait to be noticed.

'Right, Jack, I'll show you where to look for eggs and then I have to do the evening milking so you can amuse yourself till tea.'

She strides off like a man and I dash to keep up, out the back door, across the open yard and into a hay barn, a tall stone barn, open fronted with massive beams across the ceiling. She hands me a basket and we head for a rusty piece of farm machinery where a cosy hay nest has been constructed, tucked into the middle. She lifts out two golden brown eggs and pops them into the basket. Two more places to look in amongst the hay bales although there are no eggs there. Mrs Dyer collected most of the eggs this morning.

We leave the hay barn with the two eggs nestled in my basket. I stride to keep up with her as we head round the back of the barn to a large pile of dirty straw and she retrieves another egg.

'I only found this nest the other day and there were two this morning.'

She scouts around among the weeds and dry grass. 'You have to keep an eye out as they like to discover new spots sometimes.'

Next we look under some bushes at the side of the barn where the dirt is dusty and bare but there are no more eggs, just a hollow where the hens like to sit.

'They like it in here because the soil is warmed by the sun.'

Next to the barn is a huge wooden, open-sided shed with rusty-looking machinery in and next to that a stable building with a door that opens top and bottom separately. Inside, half of it looks like a proper stable with hay nets and bits of straw on the floor and lots of leather harnesses hanging on the partition wall. In the other half there are various bins with lids and she opens the nearest one taking out a scoop of corn.

'You can throw this much to the chickens each morning but make sure you close the bin and close the stable door otherwise they'll all be pecking around in here too.'

She gives me the scoop and I go outside and sprinkle the corn near the birds who come running and clucking as if I'm giving them a feast. They are rusty brown birds, all looking much the same except a bossy cockerel with glossy coloured feathers in his tail. He stands tall and looks at me suspiciously and then stands to one side checking over the hens like a headmaster.

Finally Mrs Dyer leads me to the side of a low white building with a green painted door.

'If the air raid siren goes off, you need to come down to the shelter,' she says, opening a door to a large mound covered with grass, and pointing down some dark steps.

I hope the siren doesn't go off if I'm on my own.

'The pigs and horses are along there', she says, pointing along the narrow track running alongside the shelter.

'I'll show you those tomorrow.'

I'm beginning to worry that I can't remember everything she's showing me and telling me.

Mrs Dyer has a quick look round in other nooks and crannies of the yard before telling me to take the egg basket back to the kitchen and amuse myself while she does the evening milking.

I do as she says, quite relieved to escape from her rather bossy ways, and sit at the kitchen table looking at the beautiful new eggs nestled into the basket. I'm glad I have the job of collecting eggs every day. It makes me feel quite important.

I don't know what to do now. I need to pee and can't decide whether to find a corner in the yard or try to find the toilet. There are two doors leading off the scullery that I noticed when I came back into the kitchen so I investigate them first. One of the doors leads into the coal cellar. The other one luckily houses the toilet and a huge basin streaked with rusty water marks under the tap. The toilet is high with a wooden seat and the cistern is right up against the ceiling where I can't reach the chain without climbing up on the seat.

Relieved of needing the toilet but feeling small and lonely in this faraway place on my own I make my way back to my bedroom and after a few comforting words from Oscar I curl up with him on the sea of dark green pillows and close my eyes.

CHAPTER 3

HELEN DAY

I know he can't go on working much longer. Even down to three mornings is proving too taxing. My husband who used to stride over farms in his gumboots, manhandle sheep, bring recalcitrant calves into the world, dig the vegetable patch, make love to me...' I can see him through the door now coughing into the handkerchief and finally slumping back in the surgery chair, chest heaving. The partners have been exceptionally generous, even giving me extra hours but I understand that they have advertised for a new junior partner and will have to let Gerald go soon.

My husband gathers his bag and as I tidy my desk and cover the typewriter I see him pale and drawn, walking like a man of twice his thirty five years who can hardly speak to me until he's regained his breath.

I take his arm and we walk out of the veterinary practice to the car. I drive. We only live a few minutes from the surgery and we should have sold the Morris weeks ago, but Gerald would struggle now to walk even that short distance.

'You seem worse today, my darling,' I stroke his face as he sits back on the fireside wing chair, and he nods at me, sad eyes and tight lips knowing himself that he cannot go on but reluctant to sever his last shred of normality.

'I'm going to call Dr Riches again tomorrow. You're not working so you can rest in the morning and I'll ask him to come early afternoon.'

He nods again, resigned. He's beginning to lose his positive out-
look which is an unwelcome trend and I will have to find ways of
boosting his morale, whatever Dr Riches has to say.

I hurry home, umbrella threatening to flip. The car-owners of
Petersfield all seem to be on the road today churning up the
puddles, splattering my stockings, soaking through my only decent pair of courts. Rain drips off my jacket hem into my skirt,
and as I turn into Charles Street I'm already late because I see Dr
Riches drawing up at the curb outside our gate.

I let him into the hallway before me while I pause to shake off
the brolly, and then usher him into the front room where Gerald
is already sitting poised awaiting his fate.

Busying myself in the kitchen, I try to eavesdrop on the front
room prognosis, but the door is shut and voices muted. I hope
the doctor isn't fooled by the fact that Gerald appears so much
better today after resting all morning. I know my husband will
probably play down his symptoms so I need to find an opportunity to put Dr Riches in the picture.

I needn't have worried as presently he comes through to the
kitchen, declining the cup of tea that I offer and filling his pipe
instead as he leans against the door jam. He tells me that he will
be making an appointment for another chest X-ray. He hesitates
as if he is considering his next words.

'Mrs Day, your husband is getting worse,' he pauses and raises his
eyebrow at me. 'I guess you already know that.' I nod.

'I think the best thing for him now will be to go to a sanatorium for treatment. Trouble is, with this war on there aren't so
many available beds for this sort of thing. Can you afford private
healthcare?'

We're comfortable financially but I'm wondering what sort of
sums he's going to mention.

'Em, I suppose we could afford something, but to be honest,
Doctor, things are getting tight with Gerald only working three
mornings and that will be ending very soon. We'd sell the car, of

course,' I add rather lamely.

'I'll make some enquiries and let you know. I'll notify the county medical officer and there may be a chance for your husband to have state assistance, given your circumstances.'

I make some encouraging noises. Any help will be gratefully received.

'Meanwhile, he should give up work immediately, have plenty of rest and make sure he doesn't exert himself too much. The next X-ray should give us more idea whether he needs intervention or not'.

CHAPTER 4

ELSIE DYER

Elsie Dyer scrapes down the cow pen, pushing the brown muck into the corner before shoveling the lot onto the pile in the adjoining field. Almost the last chore of the evening and she's weary. She walks briskly up the farm track, gumboots slap-slapping together and shuts the gate of the field. Fresh pasture for her fifteen Jersey cows. She leans on the three-bar gate awhile and watches their gentle grazing of the new grass. They are placid cows, each with an individual temperament that she can identify. Some special characters have names but not all. She's had to downsize the herd by nearly half since that traitorous specimen of a husband left. She even sold the bull but brought in a hired one for a while, who hopefully did the business successfully before she returned him earlier this month.

Even now it's hard on her own. With Babcock, one of the dairymen, gone to war and Curran, the other dairyman deciding he didn't want to work for a woman, it's just herself and Simmy in the morning and Bailey, the old fellow, lending a hand in the evening as Simmy has another job. Even the two young labourers have decided they didn't want to be associated with Warren Farm anymore.

She would rather be making the cheeses like she used to than milking twice a day but she can't manage that as well. A pity as cheese could be rationed soon and there will be demand again. That's if the locals can bring themselves to buy produce from her.

She rests her arms on the top bar. She's actually reluctant to return to the farmhouse, not wanting to engage with the child. What was she supposed to do with him, he's so young and doesn't appear to have much spark in him. When she was contacted about taking an evacuee - it was slightly more than a request - she asked for an older boy who could be useful. Instead they bring along this infant.

She has also put advertisements around for a room with board and lodging but as yet has not had any response. Not that she wants strangers intruding on her privacy, but money is tight. Very tight. She can't afford to take on more labour and she's struggling to keep up with the regular bills. She's had to downsize the herd in order to manage, but that of course, has meant less income from the milk. She's had to shut down the dairy too, more loss of income but the upkeep of the place never lessens. She dreads any of the herd needing the veterinary as she'd struggle with that sort of bill right now. It seemed the only option she had left was to have a paying lodger, but the thought of it makes her feel really depressed.

The sun is low, casting long purple shadows across the grass. She enjoys the evenings when the farm settles down for the night, wildflower petals close, the wind drops, birds cease their lively song. She looks out to the sea, also calm now, navy blue disappearing to the crisp line of the horizon. There is no place she would rather be, despite the endless work.

Reluctantly she leaves the cows quietly grazing and heads back to the house. The boy is probably starving by now!

The house is quiet. The boy's gas mask is still draped over the kitchen chair but he is not there, neither in the sitting room. She wanders upstairs and finds him curled up on the bed fast asleep. She feels a little sorry for him. What sort of parents send such a small child off to stay with a complete stranger. This evacuation of cities seems a heartless business.

She's not natural with small children, and has no wish to engage in a motherly sort of way with this lad, but she can still empathise with his pain.

Having never had children of her own she is wondering how she's supposed to interact with this evacuee. She might have regretted the lack of children at one stage in her life, but not now. Her teenage sweetheart, Douglas, joined the war in 1916. They promised their love eternal. They vowed to marry when she was twenty one. He spent the last months of the war in a French field hospital and returned to her as a broken man. Wheelchair bound, badly scarred both physically and mentally, he went to live with his parents and although she went there everyday to help care for him for more than a year, he eventually pushed her away saying he would not marry anyone, and she should break herself free from him. Broken hearted, she kept her hope alive for another two years when he finally succumbed to his injuries and passed away.

Looking back now, Elsie wonders just why it took her so long to heal. She resisted relationships, immersed herself working for her father in his tree nursery until, at the age of thirty five she met Arthur at the Ventnor Crab Fayre, held every June. They struck up a conversation while sitting on the seawall eating ice creams. It quickly turned into a courtship and then a proposal. He was well-known in the town, often frequented the local pubs, passed the time of day with many acquaintances although had no special friends. He was several years her senior, beginning to look his age with receding hairline greying at the temples. His ruddy and rugged complexion testament to long days in the sun, wind and cold.

With Elsie's father beginning to wind down the tree business, she married Arthur because it seemed the sensible thing to do at the time. Besides, he earned a decent living with his Jersey herd and she couldn't fault the location. She had always been a practical outdoor woman, not afraid of manual work, which she thinks Arthur was probably attracted to.

With the small capital sum she brought to the farm, they bought the tractor, baler and other machinery and had the farm connected to the electricity at last. They felt they were beginning to modernise.

There was never much romance attached to the marriage and their daily lives were quite separate, with her managing the dairy, the hens, the pigs, the kitchen garden,whereas Arthur spent his days outside with the herd and the heavy farm work. Her evenings were taken up with bread making, jam making, bottling and all the domestic chores. Arthur sat himself in the 'office' with the paperwork or, increasingly during the last year, socialising in the Crab and Lobster with his pals - or so she thought.

Five years of marriage, four months on her own and look where she is now. Tired, overworked, in debt and with an evacuee she doesn't know what to do with.

She returns to the kitchen to prepare an omelette, thinking it's a fairly safe bet that it will be something the boy will eat. She sees the egg basket on the table and is pleased there is at least one job the lad can do, but she struggles to think what else she can suggest to keep him occupied. He's such a young kid. Now the school holidays have started he will be hanging around all day. She wonders if he has any friends here. That's something she can ask him in order to make conversation.

She clatters a few pans in the hope the noise wakes the boy and then goes upstairs again to find him sitting cross legged on the bed looking into space.

'Come down and have your tea now,' she says and he nods, following her into the kitchen. He's hardly said more than two words to her since he arrived, but then she reminds herself that she hasn't said much to him either.

She places the omelette with bread and butter in front of him.

'What do you want to drink, Jack? Milk, water or tea?'

He settles for milk and when her omelette is cooked she joins him at the table.

'Have you any school friends in Ventnor, Jack?' she asks, hopeful that some friends might take the pressure off her.

He tells her that his friend Jimmy is somewhere but he doesn't know where, and a few other classmates came to Ventnor but again he doesn't know where.

She decides she will have to contact the WVS ladies to see if they can arrange something for these evacuees to meet up.

For Elsie, the rest of the evening feels like extracting blood from a stone with this boy. She has managed to discover he comes from a huge council estate in South London, that he lives with his mother, doesn't know his father, has no siblings, plays with his friend Jimmy sometimes because he has a garden but Jack only has a yard.

She is relieved when it is finally time for his bed and after making sure he can find the bathroom and reminding him to clean his teeth, she leaves him to it and sinks gratefully back in the armchair for another half hour of solitude before heading to bed herself. She has to be up at five.

Jack

I lie awake wondering if it's time to get up. The room is dark because of the thick black curtains so I slide off the high bed and peak out to the farm yard below. It is light but it feels early. I can hear the constant mooing of cows through the open window, somewhere fairly close so someone must be about.

I'm used to Mum telling me when it's time to get up, so I'm not sure what to do now.

I sit on the bed and talk to Oscar for a while, but then I need the toilet so I risk tiptoeing out to the landing, and as as I can't see Mrs Dyer moving about below I make my way down to the toilet. I'm not sure if Mrs Dyer is in or out so I wonder whether to climb up on the toilet seat and pull the chain because it makes such a noise. I do it anyway.

Mrs Dyer doesn't come so in the end I return to the bedroom, pull on yesterday's clothes and go quietly down to the kitchen. On the huge table is a loaf of bread on a wooden board, a butter dish in blue and white china and a jar of red jam. A clean plate sits there along with a dirty plate with breadcrumbs, a smear of jam and a sticky knife.

I take the hint and help myself to bread and jam. The trouble is, I've never cut a slice of bread before and have difficulty not destroying the whole loaf. It looks like a rat has been at it by the time I've finished. There is a jug of milk on the table so I find a cup upturned on the draining board and carefully pour myself a drink, which I manage without spilling any. I don't get milk at home like this and have to resist pouring myself another, but I think that might be too greedy. I wonder where Mrs Dyer is and think I ought to go and find her. It doesn't feel right to be in this strange house having breakfast all on my own. I hope if I take our plates to the sink and tidy the table it might compensate for the state of the loaf. I collect up the excess crumbs so it doesn't look quite so bad.

I head past the barn where I must collect eggs and down the farm track towards the noise I can hear. The sun is up but it feels cool with wind in my face when I look out towards the sea far below in the distance. Two brown chickens come bowling along towards me hoping for scraps but saunter off in disappointment when I clearly haven't anything to offer. I wish I'd put the breadcrumbs in my pocket for them.

I can hear the cows mooing ahead and birds singing from the hedge next to the track. I'm afraid of getting lost but if I stay on the track I should be able to return the way I came. The track is quite wide, dusty, with weeds and grass growing down the middle.

Ahead of me is a brick building with a group of cows standing in a pen outside. They look quite a lot like my farmyard cow but they are all light brown, not black and white.

This is where the noise is coming from and I presume the cows are being milked. I hang about outside the pen watching. It is an open sided building and I can see Mrs Dyer and a man sitting on stools each next to a cow, with bucket things underneath.

Presently the cows in the building are untied and let out of a gate where they amble on up the track. Two more cows step in to be milked.

I'm not sure if Mrs Dyer has noticed me or not, but they seem very busy so I pick up a stick and slash wildly at the weeds on the side of the track as I wander back to the yard.

I collect the empty egg basket from the kitchen and head for the barn. The roof is high and there's light shafting through some holes in the tiles onto the hay stacked against the back wall. I feel very scared being there on my own and it's quite dark in the corners. I'm not too sure if the chickens are friendly or not and frightened they might peck me, especially if they see me stealing their eggs. Or maybe that beady-eyed cockerel will take a dislike to me.

Two hens sit murmuring on one of the beams eyeing me suspiciously as I hunt around for eggs. Other hens are scratching around in the layer of loose hay on the floor, or outside amongst the weeds. I disturb one white-feathered hen sitting snugly in the corner of the rusty piece of machinery on a comfy nest of hay. She fastens a beady eye on me, daring me to disturb her. She may be on some eggs but I'm afraid to feel for them while she is sitting there so I leave them and decide to come back later. This feels so far from Pits Wood Estate and it feels like a very scary adventure. I wish I could share it with Jimmy.

I don't think I like it here very much. I hope I can go home soon.

CHAPTER 5

PROGNOSIS

Helen

I pull the fireside chair round so that I can sit next to Gerald who is lying on the sofa, his long legs resting on the arm. He watches me with his dark blue eyes, sandy hair pushed back off his forehead except for a certain wave that always wants to fall forward.

Dr Riches and Dr Love, the Medical Officer, have just left after bringing the result of the X-ray that I took Gerald to the hospital for on Tuesday. It is not good news.

Gerald takes my hand. 'I'm sorry, Helen', he whispers, as if it is his fault.

I pat his arm.

'We'll manage. It's just important that you are helped to re-cover, whatever it takes.'

He has an infected right lung, worse since the previous X-ray.

'How are you going to manage?' He looks at me with worried eyes. 'I could be in that place for months.'

I know Gerald feels emasculated by this disease and has seen his rightful role of main breadwinner being eroded, with his wife taking on more and more responsibility that should be his.

Dr Love has found him a place at the Royal Chest Hospital in Ventnor on the Isle of Wight. A large sanitorium for tubercu-losis patients. Although we're lucky enough to be granted state funding, we still have to find thirty shillings a week towards it. I wonder how I will afford to make regular visits, let alone pay for the bills.

'Gerald, how about this for a compromise?' I voice a thought that has just popped into my head.

'If we can rent this house for, say, six months, I could rent a cheap room in Ventnor and find a job locally. That way I could visit you every day, have enough to live on and pay the hospital bills.'

'No, our home is here and you have a good job already.'

'Well, actually I don't think it'll be long before women start to be conscripted. I can volunteer for war work on the Isle of Wight, just as well as here.'

'We can't have strangers living in our house, Helen. You could always advertise for a lodger yourself. We have a spare room. It would be company for you too.'

I can see he wants the last word on this and as he is beginning to look feverish, I let it go for now.'

I arrive early for work, hoping to catch a few minutes with the partners before their day begins.

Mr Wainwright perches on the consulting table as I update him on Gerald's illness and explain that he will not be returning to work. I tell him that I too will have to tender my resignation as I plan to move to Ventnor with Gerald.

'What about your house?'

'I shall rent it out for six months,' I tell him boldly, 'although Gerald isn't keen on the idea yet. I'm hoping he will see the sense of it when he's had time to think about it.'

He looks at me with a slight smile.

'Well, Mrs Day, you seem to have a handle on things. I'm sorry to hear Gerald's health is not improving, although that hasn't come as a surprise, and we will be much the poorer for you both leaving us. You know that we've advertised for a junior and you'll be interested to know that we've finally taken on a young veterinary, Mr Fields, starting in a week's time.'

He pauses, obviously thinking through something that has oc-curred to him.

'Now, this might be worth exploring, Mrs Day. Mr Fields is recently married and they will be looking for rented accommodation when he takes up his post, until they can afford to buy something. Perhaps I should put them in touch with you?'

CHAPTER 6

SETTLING IN

Jack

I always feel quite lonely getting up without Mum chivvying me to get a move on and I miss sitting at the kitchen table with my porridge or my toast and margarine while Mum's being busy around me, doing washing up or peeling potatoes for dinner before I'm hurried out of the door for school. Here, in my cave-black bedroom, I have to guess if it's time to get up and a couple of times I've looked through the curtains to see it's still not quite light so I've gone back to bed. I suppose it wouldn't really matter if I got up early or late because there's no one around to tell me off. I just put on the clothes off my chair and have the usual cup of stewed tea and bread and jam. I've noticed that Mrs Dyer leaves a slice of bread cut from the loaf now, after I made a mess the first time. At least she didn't get cross with me. I don't even have to bother to wash my face and no one checks behind my ears.

I usually hang around the yard and spy on the chickens to see if I can catch any laying eggs in places I don't know about. I'm afraid to wander too far because I don't know my way round the farm yet.

There are some scraps left today and Mrs Dyer says, 'Come with me, we'll feed the pigs and then that can be your job as well.'

I haven't even seen the pigs yet. We take the bowl of scraps and turn left along the narrower track beside the whitewashed building until we come to a small muddy field with a brick building in the corner.

'Wow! What's that?' I squeal. There's an enormous fat, black and pink creature lying on its side covered with drying mud. Quite hairy with big ears completely hiding its eyes. When it hears us approaching it lifts its great head, blinking at us before heaving itself to its feet. I suddenly realise it's not one but two great bulks of flesh.

Mrs Dyer looks at me surprised.

'They're the pigs, you ninny! Haven't you seen a pig before?'

I shake my head feeling very stupid. I thought pigs were small and pink with curly tails. These monsters are quite frightening the way they are slobbering and grunting as Mrs Dyer throws the scraps over the fence into the trough. I keep my distance.

Over the side fence, but backing onto the pigsty is a wooden stable and at the back of that field I can see two large brown horses grazing. I want to ask Mrs Dyer if we can pat them but after she called me a ninny I don't want to say anything stupid. Instead she just points to them and says,

'That's Pat and Biddy our two work horses,' before we walk briskly back to the stable next to the machinery barn and she scoops out a bowl of foodstuff from another of the bins and hands it to me. 'You can give the pigs this as well because there weren't many scraps. I have some work to do now. Don't forget to shut the door after you bring the bowl back.'

With that she strides up the track leaving me to face the fearsome pigs again.

Sometimes before breakfast I wander up to the milking shed and watch over the gate or I go to see the calves in the next field, but usually when they see me watching they all come running to the gate expecting their morning pails of milk and I feel bad that I'm not the one who brings them.

After the milking is all finished it is Mrs Dyer who cleans the cow yard while Mr Simmons brings the milk to the calves. It's fun to watch them jostling around the milk bucket trying to get their mouths onto the teats. Most of them know what to do but one or two bluster about and try to suck the side of the bucket or butt at it until it upturns.

Mr Simmons is quite old and sometimes he chats to me but I have to keep out of his way otherwise he gets quite irritated with me. He swears at the calves some mornings if they mess him around. He did let me ride on the tractor back to the yard one day, and that's the best thing I've done this week except for seeing Jimmy.

After the milking Mrs Dyer returns to the house with a large jug of the fresh milk and we both have porridge and I have a glass of the lovely milk. It's the best meal of the day even if she gives me too much porridge. I don't like to leave any though in case she says I'm being wasteful.

Yesterday one of the Brown Suit ladies brought Jimmy with her. I think she'd come to check up on me because she asked Mrs Dyer lots of questions about whether I'd settled in. I left them talking in the kitchen while I played in the yard with Jimmy. He's lucky. He lives in the town with a whole family and also gets to play with some other boys from our school who live nearby. I don't know why I have to be up here on my own. We played hide and seek for a while and I showed him the places where I collect eggs, then we pretended to drive the tractor. I think Jimmy was jealous of me having a real ride on it. I'd like to play at Jimmy's place but I think Mrs Dyer is always too busy to take me and fetch me.

It starts drizzling so I hang around indoors until Mrs Dyer returns for lunch. She fetches the post from the box at the end of the track. Sitting at the table she opens two brown envelopes and tuts at both of them. I think they are bills.

Everyone I know seems to be short of money or short of something or other. Some people blame it on the war but my Mum's always moaned about not having any as long as I can remember. I think it comes from not having a husband. Mrs Dyer doesn't appear to have one.

She goes to the small drawer in the drop-down cupboard and pulls out a notepad and pen and a cheque book. I sit mutely while she writes, sipping at a glass of milk to make it last.

She glances up at me. 'You can take this to the post box at the end of the lane if you like. Give you some exercise. We'll be having the bailiffs round if I don't pay this one.'

I don't really know what she means but I guess it's important. Even though it's still drizzling, I welcome the opportunity to go out.

I proudly put my new gumboots on. Mrs Brown Suit brought them with her yesterday. I think Mrs Dyer must have asked her to because she was quite exasperated with the way I was messing up my only proper shoes and coming in with caked mud right up to the laces. It wasn't easy trying to clean them properly, either. My new gumboots are not really new but they still look quite good even though they are slightly big for me. If I wear two pairs of socks they don't slop around too much.

I take the letter and wander off down the farm track to the lane. The hedges on either side are decorated with pearly spider's webs, glistening damp in the drizzle. It's really pretty. Trees drip onto the white lacy flower heads growing all along the verge. The air smells fresh and clear like washing on a line and I feel like skipping, although my boots are not the best for that so I stamp in a few muddy puddles instead.

Mrs Dyer told me to look out for motor cars when I reached the lane because there isn't a footpath. There's nothing on the road this morning, just a tractor puttering two fields away.

It's not far to the bright red post box set back into the hedge on the corner where the lane meets the main road. I pop the letter into the hole, standing on tiptoe to reach. As I stand by the post box two military motor cars come one after another down the hill towards Ventnor. I watch them pass, grey-blue with a RAF emblem on the front, and they slow down to turn into the lane leading up to the downs. From my bedroom window I can look across the fields to see the tops of tall metal masts and I suppose it's the sort of place the RAF might go. If Mrs Dyer is in the sort of mood to talk, it might be something I can ask her because most of the time I can't think what to say to her or I'm too frightened to say it.

I head back to the farm accompanied by a robin who flits from twig to twig ahead of me, occasionally bursting into song.

CHAPTER 7

CHANGE OF SCENERY

Helen

The carriage feels stuffy even though the window is slightly open and the side to side rocking and monotonous rhythm of wheels on track make me drowsy. Gerald has his eyes closed although I don't think he's asleep, even though the journey has probably exhausted him after coping with the ferry trip and insisting on carrying one of the cases to the island train.

To put it mildly we've had a few differences of opinion about letting the house in Petersfield to complete strangers, although the fact that Mr Fields is a veterinary and will be stepping into Gerald's shoes at the practice did help to mollify him a little.

If Gerald had felt more himself I certainly wouldn't have had my way, but I don't think he had the energy to argue about it anymore. In the end he reluctantly conceded that this arrangement will be more financially beneficial and he will have the benefit of regular visits from me instead of once a week or a fortnight, that's if we could keep up with the transport costs. The added journey across The Solent adds so much more time and expense to an already arduous journey.

The last fortnight has been a whirlwind. The Fields came to see us and fortunately Gerald was suitably impressed with them and we struck a mutually agreeable deal to rent to them.

I've hurriedly sorted all the paperwork, drawn up a contract, arranged the utility bill payments, cancelled the milk, organised the sale of our trusty old Morris and finally packed all our personal belongings and stored them in the loft. I feel certain our house is in safe hands.

The train slows and we are plunged into the sudden blackout of a long tunnel before emerging straight into the quaint station of Ventnor situated next to a quarry cut into the high down and overlooking the town far below. This is the end of the line and the train has steadily disgorged its many passengers as we travelled from Ryde. A small group of the many uniformed men have made it this far and instantly find a staff car waiting for them on the road outside. I wonder where they are being whisked off to.
Fortunately there are taxis waiting for hire and we bag one quickly which transports us and our luggage zig zagging down the steep and narrow streets to the coastal road heading west and on to the famous chest hospital.
I ask the taxi driver if he would collect me from the hospital in an hour to take me to a cheapish hotel to stay for the night or two in Ventnor.
Poor Gerald looks done-in after the journey, but nurse Page who is assigned to settle him into his room is all care and compassion.
I'm amazed at the size of the place, and what a fabulous setting. I think my husband is in the best place. The Victorian building is ranged in an enormously long line stretching all the way through a green and leafy valley between some high craggy and wooded cliffs and the sea. The building is made up of adjoining villas separated into two by a tall chapel.
After Gerald is settled into his own room to rest, the matron takes me on a swift tour of the villa he is in. All the bedrooms appear to be on the first floor with a large balcony stretching along the seaward side on which the patients, in their beds, are pushed each morning to breathe the beneficial sea air. Gerald's room is small but perfectly comfortable with a washbasin and a chest of drawers and as he is to be bed-bound to start with, I will

be allowed to visit at any time. I'm told that if he makes constant progress he could be there for about eight months with gradual but very regimented steps to recovery, starting with total bed rest and progressing through a few hours out of bed, right through to labouring in the outdoors in the gardens or allotments, and finally visits home.

The matron is the sort who will stand no nonsense or negotiation. She is tall and masculine, brusque but efficient. The recovery routine is sacrosanct. We have no desire to argue against it!

The afternoon is wearing on as I leave Gerald in the strict and capable hands of the nurses.

Thankfully the taxi has returned for me and I sink into it wearily along with my enormous suitcase and hold-all

The taxi driver turns to me. 'We can try the Ocean View hotel, Ma'am, if you like. If you're making regular visits to this place it's the nearest small hotel and walkable into town.'

The Ocean View is a three storey Victorian house, unremarkable, square, slightly old-fashioned and stuffy but quite adequate.

After freshening up I just have time to make an appearance in the dining room for a light tea of fish cakes and salad, finishing with a welcome cup of tea in the small sitting room where I find a local paper to browse. I scan the lodging advertisements and the jobs vacant and note a couple of telephone numbers in the back of my diary for possible places to live that I might try. Most of the jobs vacant are for carers, kitchen staff or cleaners. I hope I can do better.

I am almost ready for bed at this stage but the evening is still early, the sun still shining and the sea, which I can see clearly through the window, looks sparkling and inviting, so I muster up some last energy for a trip to town.

It is only a ten minute walk into Ventnor town along a road lined with tall terraced Victorian houses with views of the ocean at the back. These give way to the main High Street, a fairly short street that winds round in a circuit of small shops which I saunter past getting my bearings, stopping at the news-agent's window to browse the advertising cards. Another likely telephone number goes into my diary. At the next corner is a small tobacconist, also with cards in the window and I glean another possible lodging but no suitable jobs. I walk on further finding myself on a cliff path heading east out of town, but enough is enough for one day and I climb some steps up to a higher road and head back. So many Ventnor houses look precariously perched against the cliff, tucked into all manner of nooks and corners. Stepways are poked in between buildings and zig zag lanes climb up through the terraces.

On this fine evening the views are quite stunning of the cliffs marching off to both east and west.

Deciding to strike while the iron is hot to bag a suitable lodging, I locate a telephone box in the town and line up coins to make the calls. The first one I dial there is no answer. Second one and the room has already been taken. The third landlady tells me that I would have to share a room, which I don't want. The last number is the one I am least interested in as it's a farm in Upper Ventnor which I think may be too far for me to walk to the hospital each day. I ring anyway. The landlady is Mrs Dyer. She sounds as brusque as the hospital matron and assures me it takes her fifteen minutes to walk into town when I express my concern.

She tells me I had better come and see the place if I'm interested and I find myself agreeing to meet her there at 9.30 in the morning.

I place the telephone back on it's cradle and wonder if I should have given myself more time to look around but the woman on the phone sounded as if she would not countenance any indecision! The rent does seem very reasonable, though, and I don't really want to pay the Ocean View price for longer than necessary.

I stroll down the steep winding path to the seafront, marvelling at The Cascade, a natural spring falling over the rocks down to the sea.

Plenty of people are still about promenading along the front, although sadly the beach is cordoned off with scaffold poles and barbed wire. Uniformed men stroll with local girls on their arms, or stand about in small groups, smoking. There are family groups, children with ice creams and couples sitting on the benches dreaming out to sea.

After the best night's sleep for weeks and faced with a dubious breakfast of dried egg, tinned tomatoes, flaccid bacon and a brittle, oily piece of fried bread, I settle for the toast and marmalade and several cups of tea before heading to Upper Ventnor. Mrs Dyer may have been right about fifteen minutes walk down to town, but she didn't mention the hike back up again. These Ventnor people must be so fit. Everywhere is steep and winding and I'm puffing by the time I reach Chalk Lane.

Just a few more yards along and I see a sign for Warren Farm and head along the rutted track. Fortunately I wore my flat lace-ups. I stand in front of an old stone building with a roof sloping at various angles in dark red and orange tiles. There is a square bay window to the left of the thick wooden door, overhung with a pink climbing rose. Two casement windows sit to the right overburdened with the remnants of this season's wisteria.

I knock at the door but no one comes so I wander round to the back to a yard with various buildings and bits of machinery. I call out but there is nobody to be seen. The only things moving are chickens pecking around the edges of the yard.

I suppose being a farm, the workers are out in the fields doing whatever they have to do at this time of year.

The morning is pleasantly warm so I decide to wait awhile rather than disturb men at work. I wonder where the lady of the house is.

While I am standing in the yard watching a couple of bronze chickens squabbling over a scrap, I notice the back door opens a jar and a young face looks out of the gloom. I smile.

'Hello'.

The door opens wider and a boy of five or six steps into the light and stands looking at me.

'Hello', I say again.

'Hello', he says, looking at me warily, and after a pause he adds, 'are you the new lady?'

'I'm Mrs Day. What's your name?'

'Jack Patton'.

I'm slightly puzzled at that as I assumed he would be a Dyer boy.

'Is Mrs Dyer at home?'

'She said she's muck-spreading this morning.'

Now that sounds a delightful job.

'Oh, is anyone else at home?'

He shakes his head.

'Perhaps I'd better go and find her then.'

He stands in the doorway seeming to weigh up what to do next. Fair hair flopping forward over his freckled, slightly sun-pinked face, skinny legs dwarfed by baggy grey shorts and grey socks wrinkled down to his ankles.

The boy looks at me a moment longer before deciding to offer me assistance.

'Shall I show you where she is?'

I thank him and let him guide me to a track. By the time we pass a milking shed on the right all I've managed to ascertain is that he's an evacuee down from London. He marches ahead of me slop slopping in a pair of over large boots.

We come to a field and both watch over the gate where I see a man leading a horse and cart full of what is presumably the muck, and a woman forking it over the field. She looks dressed for the occasion in baggy brown trousers and a man's style check shirt, worn loose. Her hair is tied up in a floral scarf.

She looks our way, nods an acknowledgement in my direction and shouts, 'Jack, take the lady in the house,' before settling back to the task.

A strange welcome, indeed.

The boy Jack walks ahead of me again and I don't feel motivated to attempt making conversation.

The boy leads me through an outhouse, into a scullery with a large copper in the corner, a mangle, butler sink and a zinc bath hanging on the wall.

'This is the kitchen,' the boy tells me as we walk into the spacious hub of the house and I sink gratefully at the huge kitchen table.

I'm gasping for a cup of tea and really quite hungry as my morning toast and marmalade has long gone. There's a large jug of water on the side so I fill a cup and gulp it down in one.

'Was that Mr Dyer doing the muck spreading with Mrs Dyer?' I ask the boy, trying to make conversation.

'No, that was Mr Simmons. He comes to work in the mornings and another man comes in the evening to help with the milking but I don't know who he is.'

'Is Mr Dyer about?'

He shrugs. 'I don't know Mr Dyer'.

I change tack and ask him about himself and he becomes more at ease, telling me he lives with his mother on Pits Wood estate which I believe is a huge council estate in South London and that he is here 'on holiday because of the bombs'. He's been here for two weeks and has a friend called Jimmy lodging in the town with some other school friends and who's been to play here once.

When I ask him if he's been helping on the farm, he tells me proudly that his job is to collect eggs in the morning and sometimes he watches Mr Simmons feed the calves as long as he keeps out the way.

There is a hesitancy in the way he speaks as if he is weighing up his words and he wears an air of loneliness about him. He seems far too young to be evacuated here on his own and I'm surprised his mother isn't here with him.

'I expect your Mum's missing you. Have you heard from her?'

He shakes head and lightly kicks at the chair leg.

Tactless question, Helen, I realise.

Finally the elusive Mrs Dyer comes in, kicking her boots off at the threshold, wiping her hands on a piece of rag and bringing a strong smell of cow dung with her. She is taller than me and probably ten years older with a serious face and direct gaze.

'Mrs Day, I presume. Elsie Dyer. I'll show you the room and if you're happy with it we'll have some tea when I've had a wash, and talk terms.'

Gosh, even more brusque than the matron of the hospital!

I sit on a double bed with a purple counterpane and survey the room that I will probably agree to rent.

Green and cream patterned wallpaper, a fireplace with stone surround, a small dark wood bedside cupboard with matching single wardrobe and an old fashioned washstand in the corner. The window, flanked with heavy blackout curtains, looks out of the side of the house towards the high sloping downs, at the top of which sits a group of tall masts. Radio masts perhaps. I can also see the sea, flat and dark against an ultramarine sky. Seagulls wheel high up in the blue.

I'm not too sure about Mrs Dyer - not exactly unfriendly but not particularly welcoming for someone advertising for a lodger. However, there are probably far worse places to rent. This is far more spacious than a pokey spare room in someone's terraced house and I was assured there were plenty of fresh vegetables, milk and eggs, with three meals a day. That is not something to be turned down in these straightened times. The rent is reasonable too and it's still walkable to the hospital which will keep me fit.

Later, I stride back down the hill and time myself to see how long it does take me to reach the hospital. Although I don't know quite what to make of Mrs Dyer I found myself agreeing to the lodging. I had the impression that Mrs Dyer ran the place herself but she failed to mention Mr Dyer and I didn't like to ask. She told me I can have a bath once a week using the zinc bath, and can do my washing on Mondays when the copper is lit. She asked me if I could milk cows or had any other farm experience and seemed disappointed when I told her I dealt with the reception and administration for a veterinary practice. Still, if I don't

40

find any of that kind of work here, I could end up milking cows.
I find Gerald flat on his back in bed, still slightly exhausted from
yesterday's journey.

He's cheerful enough but I can see he will soon be bored to tears
lying like this all day. For the time being, though, he's content to
lie quietly and let me relate my last twenty four hours. I think
he is a little envious that I'm going to be staying on a farm and
tells me that I have to learn to milk cows if I'm going to live
there. I chatter on for about an hour but by that time his eyes are
drooping so I kiss his cheek and leave him be.

Two days later and I've settled into my room, one that catches
the morning sunrise and it's a joy to pull back the blackout curtains and marvel at the view. The wide skies with ever changing
clouds, distant sea switching colours by the minute and always
seagulls wheeling and soaring.

Mrs Dyer works all hours and keeps herself to herself, leaving me
to make myself at home.

Jack, on the other hand, seems more at ease with me now and
we've had a walk round the farm each morning after breakfast
to watch the calves, feed the pigs, and wander around the rest of
the farm to see what the horses are doing or what Mrs Dyer and
Mr Simmons are working at.

True to her word, we have eaten good food, plenty of milk and
cream on our porridge. Such a luxury. After a tea today of maca-
roni cheese with a surprisingly generous portion of cheese considering it is in short supply and expensive, I compliment her on
that very fact and she tells me she still has rounds of cheese ma-
turing in the dairy where she used to make it.

'I keep a padlock on the dairy as I don't want nosy locals coming
to help themselves,' she says, 'so don't go spreading it around
that I have cheeses.'

I think to myself that she could make a fortune on the black
market but I'm glad for our sakes she's willing to use it.

We all help to clear the dishes and I ask Mrs Dyer if I can boil hot
water. I whisper to her, 'I know it's not bath night but I think

Jack could do with a good wash', and wrinkle my nose a little.

'Oh, I see. I have noticed he's quite niffy. You'll need to put the big preserving pan on the hob. It's still got some heat.'

I'm surprised Mrs Dyer hasn't at least taken it upon herself to ensure Jack washes. She's obviously not cut out for having an infant about the place but in spite of her rather unwelcoming manner and lack of conversation I believe there may be an underlying sadness or anxiety about something. I'd still like to know where Mr Dyer is, but perhaps he's passed on or gone to war. Something stops me asking her.

'Come on Jack', I say when the water is finally hot, 'time you had a wash'.

He looks at me with those wide owl eyes as if I've said something quite extraordinary, but follows me meekly into the scullery.

He tells me his mum gives him a bath once a week in a tin bath in the outhouse and he hates having his hair washed.

'Well it will be more like a quick wash today,' I tell him, and strip him down with no further ado and dump him into the warm water that I've poured into the little bath. I wash his hair, paying no attention to grumbles, soap and rinse him all over and then leave him wrapped in a towel while I find some clean clothes.

Jack's room looks neat and tidy, hardly slept in. I see a woolly rabbit with floppy ears lounging against the headboard but nothing else to suggest it's a child's bedroom. The wardrobe is empty and nothing on the chair. I look in the suitcase on the floor under the window. It looks as if it hasn't been unpacked. Spare pants, vest and pyjamas, a grey shirt, grey shorts seen better days, grey socks and not much else except sandals, a navy jersey and a pencil case. I realise he's been wearing the same clothes for all of the two weeks he's been here. No wonder he smells unpleasantly musty.

I pop to the kitchen to ask for washing soap so I can give Jack's clothes a scrub in the water.

Mrs Dyer looks at me despondently.

'Oh dear, Mrs Day, perhaps I should have made more of an effort. I'm not used to young children and I actually asked for an older child but someone made a mistake with Jack's age and had him down as fifteen. I'm just so busy with the farm, I haven't paid him much attention.'

'I'm sure I can help out while I'm here', I say, 'and please call me Helen.'

She nods. 'Thank you, Helen.'

I return to the scullery wondering what I've let myself in for.

Jack

Things don't seem to be so bad now since that evening when Mrs Day took me off for a bath. It was so embarrassing. She even stripped all my clothes off me and I couldn't protest about having my hair washed, she just dunked me in the water then covered me in lather. I didn't even know her properly.

When Mrs Dyer is at the morning milking, Mrs Day comes to my bedroom about seven o'clock to tell me it's time to get up just like my mum does. She makes sure I have a wash and clean my teeth. I actually like someone to tell me what to do so I'm quite glad she's here. It's easier to say things to Mrs Day than Mrs Dyer too as I'm still a bit scared of her.

It was either the first or second morning while Mrs Dyer was still up at the milking shed, Mrs Day said 'Come on Jack, let's have a walk round the farm and get to know where we are living.'

It was cool outside and it was very strange because the sky was bright but a spooky mist sat over the fields so we could see the tops of trees but not the trunks, like they were floating in a white sea. It was like something in a fairytale.

We walked up the track following two light brown cows who had just left the milking shed. They weren't in a hurry and kept stopping to eat things growing at the side of the track.

We came to a rope across the track and the cows went through a gate that had been left open for them to a new field of fresh grass. We watched them a while then followed the track round a bend and back towards the farm along a narrower track, past the horses' field and their stable, but the horses were both at the top of the field and didn't come to see us. I think they like it up there.

The pigsty is next to the horses' field and has loads of weeds and dandelions growing against the walls. We stopped to look at the pigs who lay as if they were asleep in the mud, looking not at all fearsome that morning and completely ignored us. We didn't have any scraps to give them, so I had to give them a big scoop of their feedstuff later.

We stopped at the calves' field and waited for Mr Simmons to bring the milk pail. Mrs Day chatted to him and asked if I could help. He was all smiles with her, not gruff like he was with me, and I had a chance to stroke a calf and let her lick my milky fingers. He told us there was only a small amount of milk in the pail today because it was the last they were going to get. They are weaned now and don't need the milk anymore, but I could see they were pleased to have it.

When we were back in the yard, Mrs Dyer came up with the morning pail of milk for the house and Mrs Day asked her if the white building was the dairy. She told us it was where she used to make cheese.

'Why don't you make cheese now?' asked Mrs Day.

'Now I'm running this show on my own, I haven't the time for the cheese, and with only half the cows we used to have, probably not enough milk to make a profit on it. The demand tailed off as well.'

She changed the subject and led us back to the kitchen for porridge.

Over breakfast Mrs Day said, 'Would you teach us how to milk a cow while we're here if you have the time?'

That was the first time I've seen Mrs Dyer laugh, but she said she might if she's got a moment. I hope she does. I've never even seen a proper cow till now and I don't know how you milk one.

Mrs Day goes to see her husband nearly every day in the afternoons. I only found out today that she has a husband so perhaps she has more money than Mrs Dyer and my Mum.

I was thinking of my Mum this morning and wondering why she hasn't written to me and I thought she might come and see me for a while. I often wonder what she's doing. I suppose that man Bert keeps visiting. I don't think I like him much.

Mrs Day's husband is very ill, she told me, and in a hospital in Ventnor for a very long time.

When she was in town one day this week she went to Jimmy's house and arranged for me to play with him today at his house. I'm so excited.

I walk with Mrs Day down the lane and she chats about the weather which is cloudy and windy today, and she notices the robin leading us along again. It's easy to be with Mrs Day and I don't feel I have to say something or be quiet. It's alright either way. I look at her from the side and think she's quite pretty. Her hair is dark and shiny, just long enough to reach her shoulder in bouncy waves. She wears red lipstick. My Mum never wears lipstick and Mrs Dyer doesn't either. She offers her hand to me and I take it. It feels safe and homely.

Jimmy lives in a terraced house in a side street near the town. The lady who owns it, Mrs Price, is a really friendly lady, short and round with tight curly brown hair. Jimmy calls her Aunt Clarice. She gave me orange squash and a homemade biscuit before Jimmy and I went out to play on some swings on the green near the back of their house. It's right on the cliff top so you can see way out to sea, especially if you swing high and it feels like you are flying up with the seagulls.

When Mrs Day collects me at the end of the afternoon I think the sun and fresh air have made me brave because I tell her, 'Jimmy calls Mrs Price Aunt Clarice. Can I call you Aunty Helen?'

She smiles a red-lipped smile and takes my hand. 'Yes, why not!'.

CHAPTER 8

AIR RAIDS

Helen

Monday August 12th. Eight days. I've walked into Ventnor in the last six mornings and trailed around shops and eateries looking for work. I've put cards everywhere that takes them offering work of bookkeeping, typing and general office work but with no luck yet. I've written letters with my CV to the schools, the GP surgery, the local council. I fear our savings will not last long at this rate.

In the afternoons I walked the mile to the Royal Chest Hospital to visit Gerald.

My poor love is still on the total bed rest regime at the moment and that means he is not even allowed to sit up in bed to eat his food. He tries to be cheerful when I visit but I can see he is bored and fed-up.

I bring him a newspaper to read on each visit, and although I've brought books for him to read he complains he can't concentrate on them and it's too difficult to read a paper when flat on his back. I find myself urging him to be patient during this phase and when the consultant next comes, if nothing has worsened, Gerald should be able to sit up in bed and maybe spend an hour in the chair each day soon after that. It must be a very tedious time for him even though the hospital itself seems so professionally run and the nurses all very kind. He is waiting for the next X-ray to find out if his lung is any worse.

Whatever the temperature he is out on the balcony in his bed, or if it's raining hard he is pushed to the large French doors which are thrown open to the strong ocean air from which he is encouraged to breathe deeply. The doors are never closed, even at night.

I've learnt my lesson to bring a warm jersey with me, as it can be quite cool sometimes if there is a wind off the sea. I wonder what it will be like in the winter but the nurse assured me that Ventnor has a very mild climate as it is sheltered from north winds by the high Boniface Downs. Even so I don't suppose it will feel tropical in the middle of January.

The hospital itself is set in a dip between the cliff to the north and the sea to the south. The extensive gardens are surrounded by trees keeping the worst of the chill winds at bay and contributing to the mild climate.

From Gerald's balcony I usually see men working in the grounds below, pushing a barrow, raking leaves, planting in the vegetable garden and so on. Much of their food is produced on site. It's quite a little farm, in fact. I look forward to the time when Gerald is well enough to do a little of this outdoor work because that will mean his next step will be home. We have a long way to go yet, though, so I shouldn't get ahead of myself.

A couple of mornings this week, I took Jack into town with me so that he could play with his friend and one day Mrs Price brought Jimmy to the farm where they spent the morning being farmers on the tractor and climbing the hay bales in the barn.

I think it has done Jack good to have some child company and he seems more cheerful.

Right now he is off to do his important job on the farm of feeding the chooks and collecting the eggs. He is rightly proud of his daily contribution to the table and, goodness, how wonderful it is to eat fresh eggs again. I cannot take to the awful dried stuff at all.

I think I will mention to Mrs Dyer again that it would be fun if she could show us how to milk a cow. If I could do that, perhaps I could help her with the milking sometimes. It would be good to have something to do here while I try to find some work, and Mrs Dyer does seem to be overloaded running the place mostly alone. She's a strange one. Quite abrupt at times, always appears to me as if she has much on her mind.

I busy myself in the kitchen clearing the table of the bread and jam, and put a pot of porridge on the slow hob until she's finished the milking.

She comes in with the pail of milk and a waft of cow muck. She holds two or three letters from the box, one of which she hands to me.

'Another for you, Helen,' and she sits at the other end of the table slitting open her two brown envelopes with a deep frown on her brow and a loud sigh. Obviously not welcome post for her.

I open mine with little optimism which is just as well. The last of the vacancies I wrote for has already been filled. I wonder what to do now. The savings won't last long and I'm afraid Gerald may have been right that I should have stayed in Petersfield. Trying to hide my disappointment, I serve out the porridge for us all and although I was reluctant at first to tread on Mrs Dyer's toes, so to speak, I believe she welcomes any small help she receives to relieve her burden of work.

I noticed that there is a small, rather weed-ridden kitchen garden at the back of the dairy with various vegetables and herbs struggling through the grass and bindweed. I ask her if Jack and I can spend some time sorting it out and perhaps plant some new vegetables to last into the winter. It was something I thought we could do in the mornings to keep him occupied - and me.

She looks enlivened by that idea.

'Good idea. I've neglected it these last few months even though the Ministry wants everyone with land to grow their own. They tell me I must grow a certain acreage of spuds for the war effort too, but I can't do everything. I've harvested all the earlies out that back field but I'll soon have to start getting the main crop in. Just hoping Simmy can help again.'

'Can you get some land girls in to help?' I ask her.

'Can't be having prissy young city girls here, afraid to break a nail. I need a strong pair of hands. Besides, they'd have to stay at the hostel in town and that'll be a hotbed of gossip that I can do without'.

I decide not to argue but press on with a change of subject while she appears willing to chat, and ask her again about showing us how to milk.

'Well, if you sort out the garden for me, I'll teach you how to milk a cow. We can do it next Sunday when I'm not so busy.'

I offer to walk into town to buy some essentials as I also want to see if there are any seeds available worth planting this late. I know Mrs Dyer hates queuing at the shops and avoids venturing into town if she can possibly manage without it. I take Jack with me.

Summer has warmed up and under a cornflower sky with temperatures in the mid seventies we walk hand in hand jauntily down the winding road and steep steps into town.

I wear my yellow floral dress with the cap sleeves, and walk hatless. Jack has his usual grey flannel shorts and grey shirt with the sleeves rolled up. He looks hot already and I decide to call into the WVS office to see if they can give me a summer shirt for Jack. They usually have a small supply of donated clothes for evacuee children.

The town is bustling with gossiping women and groups of military personnel smoking and watching them.

Even though we are way past the early rush the queues of patient women are long. I join the butcher's line and smile at the woman in front.

'Hello. I noticed you in town the other day', she says in a friendly way. 'Are you new around here?'

'Yes. I'm staying at Warren Farm in Upper Ventnor.'

'Warren Farm?' she says with a frown. 'With Mrs Dyer?'

I confirm that that is so.

'You a relation or something?' She sounds less friendly now.

'No, I'm lodging there. My husband is at the chest hospital so I'm here for a few months while he's recovering.'

She turns back to the woman in front of her who is listening to our conversation and they give each other a look.

The first one turns to me and says fairly brusquely, 'well, I'm sorry to hear about your husband and hope he recovers soon.'

She turns her back and the two in front gossip quietly among themselves ignoring me completely.

I feel slightly rebuffed and try not to engage with anyone else in the queue.

I finally manage to secure a package of scrag end of lamb before heading to the greengrocer and another queue.

I decide to keep my own counsel in the greengrocer line and the women are somewhat more friendly. I don't mention Warren Farm.

After our visit to the greengrocer I call into the WRVS office and leave feeling very satisfied. With more than a little wheedling from me I come away with an aertex shirt, a cotton short sleeved shirt that looks too big, but better than nothing, and a pair of khaki shorts. Jack hops and skips out onto the pavement, obviously as chuffed as I am.

As we walk towards the Coop for the last of the shopping the air raid siren wails through the town. People start to hurry along the street towards the shelter. Several people stand, shielding their eyes from the sun, watching through a gap in the buildings the approaching threat.

Strung out across the channel a massive flock of stiff, black crow-like planes gathers menacingly towards us. The sky is dark with looming trouble. It looks like hundreds of planes heading our way and the drone of the engines starts to drown out the noises of the town.

People are now dashing down the High Street, mothers dragging their reluctant children and some of the military staff encouraging people to hurry. Someone nearby says, 'planes are flying high. Reckon Portsmouth's in for that lot.'

We slow our pace to a smart walk when suddenly a group of low-flying German bombers come screaming over the rooftops, machine-gun fire spitting ricochets off the brick and concrete. Jack screams. People around us dive for cover in the doorways, shrapnell showers around us and I push Jack onto the step of the antique shop where we cower against the wall.

Bombs start exploding above us and around us. The ground reverberates with each crash and the air fills with dust and flying debris. My throat is soon choked, my ears ringing. The sky is criss-crossed with roaring planes dive-bombing the town. People are screaming, rat-tat of machine guns, glass splintering and cascading over the pavement.

An almighty explosion actually lifts my body off the ground with a force I could not have imagined, depositing me in a winded heap on the pavement. Feeling temporarily deafened and blinded I grope in the debris for Jack, grabbing his sleeve and tugging him to my side. His piercing screams cut into my deafness. Glass explodes on top of us showering us with deadly shards, and for seconds I am completely disorientated, wondering if we have simply died. A great grey cloud engulfs us, choking off our air.

Gasping, I look down to see Jack's face covered in blood which is streaming from a deep gash in his head. He's still screaming with fright, tears mingling with the blood and dust.

I grope in my pocket for a handkerchief that I wad over the wound, although such a small piece of flimsy cotton is nearly useless.

'Hush now, hush. You'll be fine.' I cradle him in my arms.

The air is still full of the sounds of planes and gunfire, although most of the explosions now are echoing down from Boniface Down and I think the bombers must be aiming for the military site. Not for the first time I wonder exactly what goes on up at the RAF station. I can't even see the downs now for the black smoke.

I stand on shaking legs and hoist Jack onto my hip even though he weighs almost more than I can safely carry, and we scramble over the mess of concrete, rock, tarmac and window-glass trying to find our way through. Jack is clinging like a limpet to me, eyes streaming and blood still oozing down his face, soaking into his shirt and the front of my dress.

I struggle with him across the road, my hearing gradually returning to the sound of screams and cries all around us, more distant rat-tat of gun fire and more mighty explosions high up on the downs which sends us all diving for the ground again.

Jack is crouched under my arm shaking with fear and I stand up tentatively checking we are both in one piece.

There is a strange moment of eerie quiet after the planes retreat and the choking dust settles, before the town erupts to the clanging of bells, wails of sirens, people shouting, feet hurrying, falling masonry.

With my legs feeling weak and shaky, I pull Jack upright. He looks at me with wide terrified eyes and seems unable to speak. His cheeks are streaked with grey and red where wet tears have carved runnels through the dust and blood. My hands are trembling uncontrollably and I discover I'm also bleeding from various cuts along my arms and a split lip. I lift Jack onto my hip again and venture along the street, picking my way over the piles of glass and rubble.

I can see the front half of the Coop is reduced to a roofless shell, splintered wood, shards of glass poking menacingly from broken window frames, paper fluttering off the walls and a mess of goods scattered throughout. I realise we could have been inside when the bomb hit.

'Can I help you, lady?'

A man offers to carry Jack for me.

'I can see you've got a war wound there, laddy,' he says as I release Jack gratefully into his arms.

Jack, however, clings desperately to me, until I keep hold of his hand tightly and the three of us work our way down the High Street where there is a Red Cross vehicle parked and medical volunteers tending to the walking wounded.

I thank our good Samaritan and hand Jack to the ministrations of the nurse.

I sit with Jack on my lap while his head is patched with a fat wad of dressings and a bandage wound round the lot. He is still whimpering, I'm not sure if it's with pain or shock, or both.

I can't carry him all the way back up to the farm so I have to cajole him to walk.

Emergency services are struggling through the chaos and wardens and soldiers hurry people down the street away from the scene.

We struggle up the steps to the upper road where military personnel are stopping all traffic except emergency vehicles and turning pedestrians away.

I have to explain where we are heading and an officer waves us through.

It feels like it takes us for ever to reach as far as Downs Lane, where dozens of military vehicles and personnel are turning out of the RAF camp onto the main road, many looking as dishevelled and shocked as ourselves. A dark pall of smoke hangs over everything.

Elsie Dyer

Elsie puts a pot of beans, potatoes, turnips and onions into the bottom of the range to cook slowly for the rest of the morning. It will save her time later.

She has to admit she was very concerned about their safety when the bombs started flying. It was quite unexpected really. She rarely bothers to dash for the shelter these days. More often than not the planes go sweeping overhead towards more important targets, mainly London, although that appears to have eased off a little. Of course it's not infrequent that some cowardly pilots offload their deadly cargo before they have to face the barrage from anti-aircraft guns across the Solent, but she's usually too busy to sit around in the dark shelter twiddling her fingers waiting for the all clear.

She heard the siren wailing up from the town and looking out to sea she was quite shocked at the sheer number of bombers massing towards them. Assuming as usual they were heading for the mainland cities it was with some surprise to hear the screams of low-flying aircraft and bombs suddenly raining down just a stone's throw away.

Simmy had just left after they had spent half the morning erecting a new field fence and she was piling the wire and fence posts into the trailer when the first bombers broke from the main flock, letting loose their fury on the town below.

The mass of planes continued to fly in great waves overhead but when explosions started hitting the downs it felt too close for comfort and she cowered down beside the pigsty wall, being the nearest solid structure around, half expecting a rogue bomber to demolish her farmhouse. She'd left it too late to dash for the shelter.

British fighter planes came swooping in to intercept but the bombs and planes kept raining down. One bomb fell so close she felt part of the pigsty fall on top of her and the ground literally bounced underneath her. She heard a shocked cry escape from her mouth as she covered her head with her hands and the air was filled with smoke and dust. She was certain the bomb was on her land.

The mayhem kept her crouched low on the ground for a good quarter hour before the planes veered away and the ringing in her ears was replaced with the discordant choir of mooing and bellowing from further up the farm track.

She rose shakily to her feet feeling bruised and scratched from falling pieces of pigsty, and was surprised to see the pigs had hunkered down on the other side of the pigsty and didn't look the least bit perturbed.

Across the fields towards the top of the downs a pall of black smoke hung. She could hear emergency vehicles in all directions.

With her legs feeling weak with shock she made her way up to one of the middle fields to the herd, expecting half of them to have jumped the fence or hedge in fright. The cows were bunched into a huddle in the far corner of the field noisily voicing their displeasure and fear. She leant on the gate calling quietly to them, partly to calm her own jangled nerves than those of the cows, and gradually a few braver beasts resumed their leisurely grazing.

Reassured she walked right round the farm, checking. The calves were also bunched into a huddle in the far corner but seemingly unharmed.

By the time she came to one of the top fields the air was still foggy with dust and it was clear it had been blasted by a bomb. Clods of soil and divots sprayed outwards from a deep hole in the ground, almost against the back fence which was flattened and half buried in the loose earth.

She worried then about the horses in the next but one field and hurried on to find them nervous and restless in their field stable. She tried to pacify them but they were so on edge she was afraid of being kicked. Hurrying back to the yard, with another glance at the pigs who appeared much less agitated than the horses, she grabbed some fresh hay and a couple of gnarled carrots from the garden and jogged back to the horses to coax them into a calmer state.

At least the house was still standing, she thought, wondering just how much damage the Germans had wreaked on their RAF neighbours. It triggered some worrying thoughts.

Helen and Jack were still not home and as the minutes ticked by she became more and more concerned about them. She spent the afternoon trying to keep busy but all the time she was keeping an eye out in the hope of seeing them walking into the yard.

By mid afternoon she was so anxious she was trying to think what she should do about them, so it was with huge relief when she spied her two lodgers coming, exhausted, into the yard, Helen struggling with the effort of carrying Jack and both covered in grey dust, blood-soaked clothes and bruised and scratched faces between them, Jack sporting a padded bandage around his head.

They brought a tale of chaos and destruction in town and they both sat at the table looking white-faced and stunned. Elsie set the kettle on the stove while Helen related their experience and consequent help from the Red Cross.

Both were badly shaken after their lucky escape from the fated Coop and even after they all shared a calming pot of tea Jack stayed glued to Helen's side for most of the evening. He didn't say a word until much later when he asked if the bombers were going to come back.

They were all very subdued when they gathered around the wireless later on to tune in to the Home Service as they usually did at that time. There was a mention of the raid on Ventnor Town and a blitz on the docks at Portsmouth but nothing said of the RAF station.

This next day has dawned damp and windy. There were no more air raids overnight and although Jack still seemed a little quiet over breakfast he is pleased that he has an injury to show for his ordeal. Helen was slightly worried in case the chest hospital had been hit but Elsie tried to reassure her that it was mainly the RAF station the bombers were interested in.

She and Simmy are ploughing the top field today. Fortunately they managed to get the hay in while the weather was dry a few weeks ago with some extra help from Simmy's nephew and a friend of his who are not quite old enough to enlist. The hay baler makes the job so much easier than it was in past years, and with labour being hard to find now, it's a godsend. She even hires the baler out to other farms which brings in a little cash. This was her money well spent, she thinks.

They have another task to sort out now, she considers ruefully, thinking about the fence in the top field to replace and the paddock to put back to some semblance of order now there's a huge crater in its midst.

Weather rarely stops a farmer she muses as she tugs on her tough gum boots. Even Helen said she'd lend a hand this morning but as she hasn't any experience handling heavy horses there's not much Elsie can think she can do to help in the field. Also, Elsie thinks she's still a little shaken after her experience yesterday, as she's more subdued than she usually is. Instead she suggested

Helen make the bread and the dinner for the day which will save Elsie some time later.

She's quite impressed with what Helen and Jack achieved in the kitchen garden, especially as they managed to uncover the marrow and the tomato plants that were slowly being choked by the bindweed.

She thinks about what Helen suggested regarding land girls. Although she recognises she needs more help, she hates the thought of even more folk intruding on her life. They would have to live in the hostel in town and she's sure that is a den of local gossip which she doesn't need.

Helen paid her rent yesterday which she's thankful for, helping her to pay off some of the mounting bills, which she never seems to have time to deal with. The pile of paperwork on the kitchen table grows higher each day. She knows that Helen is concerned about money too, having had no luck with finding a job. She supposes she has to pay towards her husband's treatment and guesses that could be a costly outlay.

She toys with the idea of offering Helen a reduction in rent if she could deal with all the paperwork as that seems to be her field of expertise, but she's not sure she wants a relative stranger knowing her affairs, or how much she must be in debt.

She also admits that Helen has a much better way with the lad and is relieved to have that burden lifted from her. He certainly appears happier now that Helen is here and she's noted, with a slight tinge of envy, how he calls her Aunty Helen. She guesses that 'Aunty Helen' has become a substitute for his absent mother, who, she considers is sadly lacking in maternal responsibility as she hasn't even made contact yet.

Helen

'Darling, I was worried about you.'

Gerald is sitting up in the bed propped by several pillows as he holds his arms out in welcome and I kiss him.

'They tell me the town was hit and the RAF station on the downs. I hope you were alright up on the farm.'

'Yes, we were all fine,' I tell him, preferring not to mention that we'd been caught up in it. He would only worry and say I should have stayed in Petersfield.

'I couldn't come and see you yesterday because of all the activity but it's wonderful to see you are sitting up. How are you feeling?'

A bout of coughing and a while to catch his breath tells me that Gerald is not out of the woods yet, but he smiles and says at least he isn't feeling worse.

Gerald's bed has been placed at the open French doors, but just undercover as it's raining in earnest this afternoon and I sit next to the bed with the south wind blowing the dampness over me. I accept it as a small inconvenience compared with Gerald's lot.

'What have you done to your lip?' he asks, touching the cut on my mouth, which thankfully is relatively minor.

'Oh just banged it on a bit of machinery in the barn. Nothing to worry about.'

I change the subject.

'Guess what I've been doing this morning, Gerald. Making bread! Can you believe it?'

As I'm not the best cook in the world and never make bread, my husband rightly shows some surprise.

'Heavy as a house brick?' he asks.

I flick playfully at him.

'Actually it was quite acceptable even if I say so myself.'

He laughs and gives me a hug.

It's such a relief to find him in good spirits for a change. He seems more interested in the things I talk about so I describe life at the farm and how Mrs Dyer works all hours because, for some reason she seems reluctant to talk about, her husband is no longer there and other workers have gone to war.

'I wouldn't mind helping out on the farm sometimes for something to do in the mornings but I fear I'd be more of a hindrance than help. Mrs Dyer did say she'd teach Jack and I on Sunday to milk a cow, so that should be fun.'

Gerald, who knows exactly how to milk cows, hangs his hand down like an udder and instructs me how to squeeze his fingers like a teat. All very well until we collapse with laughter sparking off another coughing fit. Unfortunately this time it brings the nurse bustling into the room with a scowl in my direction and a good deal of fussing with Gerald's pillows, waiting patiently at his side until his breathing returns to normal.

'I think it's time you rested now, Mr Day.' She looks pointedly at me. 'Five more minutes.'

I don't argue. They run an extremely tight ship here.

Before I leave, Gerald asks about my job-hunting progress, expressing concern for our finances. I've already placed more cards around town offering administration or bookkeeping although I don't feel too optimistic of results. I reassure Gerald that I'm managing fine for now, although privately I wonder how long that will last. I fear I may soon be serving teas in a cafe or mopping floors in some institution.

The following day, I receive a letter.

From Hugh Taylor, Downend Farm.

He invites me to contact him regarding an interview for bookkeeping of the farm finances and accounts. It will only be one morning a week, but at least it's a start.

'Where is Downend Farm, Mrs Dyer?'

'Just along Downs Lane. Not far. Our furthest field to the south is on their boundary.'

'Do you know them?' I wonder if they are friends of hers as they are close neighbours.

'Hugh and Molly Taylor. I know them. Only in passing though. Used to see them more but not now'.

I wait for her to explain but she busies herself at the sink. Sometimes I wonder if Mrs Dyer has any friends.

I decide to call on Mr Taylor before I walk down to the hospital to see Gerald this afternoon.

That simple task proves to be complicated trying to persuade two armed officers manning a makeshift barricade across Downs Lane.

'Can't go up there Ma'am.' I'm told.

I explain that I need to reach Downend Farm.

After further exchanges one of them turns to a field telephone to make a call to superior officers.

Finally I'm allowed through under escort from a junior officer.

Although the farm track is just a short way along the lane, I can see plainly that bomb craters are everywhere I look and I pick my way carefully along the drive to the farmhouse.

Hugh Taylor has a likeable, jovial nature and greets me with enthusiasm. He's as tall as his wife is short, about fifty years old with bushy, greying hair and an outdoor complexion. It seems that, like Mrs Dyer, they have lost their farm labourers and with their own increased workloads the farm books have been neglected.

I look briefly through their pile of paperwork, stacking up on the sideboard in the dining room. Outstanding bills for feedstuffs and the veterinary. Invoices, receipts, circulars, quotes. Wages to pay. All stuff I'm quite familiar with.

'So, Mrs Day, you're lodging at Warren Farm. What brings you to Ventnor?'

I explain about Gerald being in the chest hospital and that I answered Mrs Dyer's advertisement for a lodger.

'What do you think of Mrs Dyer, then?'

It needs a little caution and diplomacy to answer such a question. I've already discovered that the Taylors and Mrs Dyer are not close friends at the moment. I give a vague answer.

'I haven't had much time to know her very well yet. She certainly works hard and she feeds us well.'

'Us?'

I tell him about Jack being evacuated from London.

'I believe Mrs Dyer requested an older boy who could work on the farm, but it seems someone muddled the ages. Jack is only five!'

Mr Taylor laughs.

'I bet that upset her! Heard anything about her husband?'

It seems to me that Mr Taylor is fishing for information.

'No, Mrs Dyer doesn't talk about him. Has he gone to war?' Perhaps I'm fishing too!

'Ha,' he scoffs. 'Nothing so patriotic. Best you hear about him from Mrs Dyer, though, or I'll be accused of tittle tattle.'

He changes the subject and talks about the bombing raid on the RAF station further up their lane.

'All hell was let loose up here. Bombs exploding all around us. We've had several bombs land in our top fields. Made a real mess of them and blasted the hell out of our potato field. Molly and I hid in the cellar. Just thankful our buildings are still standing although the windows at the side are all blown in. Had to do some emergency boarding up this morning.'

Mrs Taylor appears in the doorway, wiping her hands on a teacloth.

'And guess who had to sweep all the glass up. Everywhere, it was.'

'Couldn't move for military and emergency vehicles and top brass showing up in their posh motors. I think they've evacuated everyone who was working up there. There must have been casualties. There's still all manner of comings and goings.'

'What exactly goes on up here?' I guess there's something important to do with the war effort for Mr Hitler to send his bombers.

'It's all top secret and no one's too sure, but we think it's some sort of early warning system. All very hush hush. I expect Mrs Dyer knows more than she lets on.'

Hugh Taylor walks me to the farm entrance.

'What day can you start?'

We agree on me starting in the morning and then every Thursday thereafter. It's a small step. I just need a few more opportunities like this.

Jack

I had a brilliant day yesterday. I thought it was going to be spoilt because it had been so miserable the day before, but when I looked out the window in the morning the sun was up chasing away some early mist and then it became hotter as the day went on. Even the sea in the distance was already sparkling by the time I had my breakfast and I couldn't wait for Aunty Helen to get herself ready.

She looked very smart in a red spotted dress with a swingy skirt and her dark hair rolled neatly like mini Swiss rolls. She does paperwork for a nearby farm on Thursday mornings, but she promised to walk down to the steps with me before work.

Jimmy and his Aunty Clarice met me at the bottom of the steps because we were all going off to the beach. I was so excited. Mrs Price works at the laundry but it's closed on Thursdays so she said she would take Jimmy and her two boys, Laurie and Don, and me to the beach.
Aunty Helen has taken the bandage off my head and instead I have a large, thick plaster over the wound. She said I mustn't put my head under the water and should just paddle.
Mrs Dyer just laughed.
'Salt water won't hurt him,' she said.
My head hurt a lot when it was cut and I was really frightened in the bombing. It's a pity I can't show off my bandage because it doesn't look so injured anymore but I expect Jimmy will still be impressed.
Most of Ventnor beach has barbed wire along it and a barrier of scaffolding poles put there to stop the Jerries landing but there's a small section round the bay that people can use. We carried our picnic and bags through the town, passing the place where Aunty Helen and I had to shelter from the bombs. The coop shop, what's left of it, is boarded up and there's a big tarpaulin over the roof. There's still lots of rubble and glass about so we had to be careful. Men were making repairs all over the place.
We found the patch of beach where we were allowed to swim

and Mrs Price spread a blanket over the shingle. We shed our shoes and socks and then our shirts. I only have my grey school shorts on but Mrs Price brought me a pair of Laurie's swimming shorts to wear. It was all a bit embarrassing when she held up a towel for me to change behind, but I had to look grateful. It was even worse when I found the shorts were miles too big and I had to pull the waist cord in so much they looked like a skirt.

The two Ventnor boys ran straight down to the sea and plunged in with whoops and shouts, turning to holler to Jimmy and me to hurry up. Jimmy soon ran down to join them but I didn't feel as brave as him. I can't swim and I've never been in the sea before. I stood at the edge watching the waves as they raced up the beach leaving a foamy edge that disappeared into the shingle. The water felt freezing on my bare feet.

'Come on in, Jack,' they shouted and one of them splashed a huge wall of water over me and then all of them laughed as I screamed with the shock of it. Not wanting to appear a scaredy custard I jumped up and down in the waves until I was wet all over, trying not to shriek. To my surprise, after a few minutes, the water didn't feel so cold and I started to have fun splashing about with Jimmy. He can't swim either but the other two can and I wish I could swim like them.

With every wave I was in danger of losing my shorts but at least no one could see while I was in the water.

It was colder when I came out the sea than when I was in and I shivered under a towel for a while until it was picnic time and Mrs Price handed round some spam sandwiches. I'm not keen on spam but better than my Mum's fish paste any day.

It felt lovely to bury my bare feet into the shifting shingle and feel hot sun on my shoulders.

We played games of five stones, threw pebbles at a white rock to see who could hit it first and splashed around in the sea again. By the time we left the beach I felt really tired and when Aunty Helen came to collect me we had to trudge all the way up that long hill back to the farm. I fell asleep on the sofa before we even had our tea.

Today is hot again. I collected the eggs and fed the pigs. I don't mind Dotty and Flo now - they are the pig's names - as they never do very much except sleep in the mud or the dust. Mrs Dyer told Aunty Helen that Dotty had eight baby piglets not long ago but they were all sold just before we arrived. She said Dotty is pregnant again but I don't know how that happens.

Aunty Helen was excited this morning as someone put a note through the door from the farmer she went to see yesterday. He asked if she'd like to call on a friend of his, a farmer in the next village, who might want her to work for him in the same way.

She had to catch a bus as it's quite a long walk, so I'm amusing myself the rest of the morning while Mrs Dyer and Mr Simmons finish ploughing the top field.

I decide to wander up the track to watch the horses working although I'll have to keep out the way because Mr Simmons can have a bad temper sometimes and even Mrs Dyer can be cross if I'm a nuisance.

My feet are really hot and sweaty in these gumboots but I'm afraid of getting my school shoes too mucky even though the ground has dried out since Tuesday.

I watch through the bars in the gate. At one point the horses and plough drive right down the edge of the field where I'm standing. Mrs Dyer is at the head of the horse on the other side from me. I'm not sure if she can see me. The horses are huge and I can almost reach through the gate to touch their lovely shiny brown coats like fresh conkers. I can hear them blowing and snorting, the clink clink of the harnesses and I catch their horsey smell as they plod past, their large round hooves, curtained with long white hair, keeping a straight line next to the previous furrow.

Mr Simmons comes last, puffing, guiding the plough as it digs into the soil curling it over like a wave in the ocean. I climb up on the third bar of the gate in order to watch their progress up the field.

Suddenly, as they turn at the top the air raid siren wails out from below. I freeze, standing on the gate not knowing what to do.

I'm frightened. Mrs Dyer and the horses just carry on as if they haven't heard. I don't know whether to stay where I am or even if they know I'm here. In my fright I stand up on the bar of the gate and shout.

'Mrs Dyer! What shall I do?'

After a few seconds she stops the horses and trudges over the furrows towards me.

'Run back to the shelter, Jack. We'll join you in a few minutes.'

I hesitate. I don't want to run back on my own.

'Go on!' She urges. 'The torch is just inside the door.'

I jump down from the gate and run along the track towards the house. It's quite a long way from the top field. I can hear the drone of planes now and a glance to my left across the fields toward the sea I can see the dark silhouettes looming closer looking as if they are heading straight for us. My breath comes in sharp panicking gasps as I run into the yard.

I pull open the low door of the shelter and feel for the torch, my hand fumbling to switch it on. I'm afraid to step down into that dark space on my own and tears of fright spring unwanted down my cheeks.

Feeling my way carefully down the steps I sit huddled on the bench unable to stop my sobs of fear and feeling like a baby. I don't want Mrs Dyer or Mr Simmons to see me afraid.

The roar of planes sounds louder and I cover my ears. Even with my hands blocking out the sound I can hear and feel the planes approaching, followed by muffled explosions, one after another as the bombs come raging down. It all sounds so close. Every time a bomb hits the ground I feel the earth shaking through to my bench and all the bits and pieces in the shelter are jiggling around on the shelf.

This is terrifying. It's worse than being with Aunty Helen in the town. I squeeze my eyes shut trying to block everything out but I can hear myself crying even though I'm not aware that I am. It goes on forever. One terrific crash sounds so close I let out a scream and all sorts of dust and debris come showering over me. I crouch over the bench, hands over my head and eyes screwed tight.

Eventually the bench stops jumping. I can hear the roaring of aircraft right overhead but then becoming dimmer. All becomes quiet but I'm afraid to move. The torch is still on and I worry in case Mrs Dyer says I've wasted the batteries. I switch it off but I panic in the sudden dark and fumble to switch it on again but I'm all fingers and thumbs and for a minute I'm terrified I'll be left in the blackness of this awful place.

A siren wails out. Does this mean All Clear or does it mean more planes are coming. I'm not too sure. I stay where I am and hope somebody comes. No one does.

Eventually I calm down a little and wipe my cheeks with my hand. I creep back up the steps, push open the door and squint against the glaringly bright light in the yard. Nothing out there seems to have changed. I walk across the yard to the hay barn and sit on one of the new bales. I don't know why but I can't face going into the farmhouse on my own right now. I just want someone to come.

Elsie

Elsie draws back the blackout curtains and looks out at the dawn. Already promising a fine day, a wispy mist floating over the fields and the sky steadily lightening in the east. She yawns.

It had been a hot and restless night with uncomfortable thoughts marching jack-booted through her mind for much of the night, not least about her own failings.

She let the boy down yesterday afternoon, she realises that. Sometimes she just forgets he's only five. At the time she thought she was doing the right thing sending him back to the shelter, given the air raid on Monday was so close, but she couldn't go with him because of the horses. She couldn't risk them taking fright while shackled to the plough and she couldn't leave Simmy to cope alone. What could she do? She'd had to unshackle them and run them back to the stable, by

66

which time the planes were already low overhead and a barage of bombs decending over the downs, with the ground shaking beneath their feet and the horses bucking against the rein.

She and Simmy needed to lie low during the raid, hunkering down against the pigsty where Elsie sheltered just a few days earlier. By the time she felt it was safe enough to make her way back to the house, Jack was nowhere to be seen. She eventually found him huddled in the hay barn, visibly shaken.

He'd obviously been crying and wouldn't speak to her. She tried to cheer him up and took him into the kitchen for a hot milk and piece of cake but he picked half-heartedly at his cake before he said he was tired and went upstairs to bed.

Helen returned soon after and Elsie was relieved to leave her to see to the lad while she returned to the fields to check on the livestock, top up the horses' hay nets and make sure they were calm.

If it wasn't for Helen being here, she would definitely try to have Jack re-housed. She knows she is just not cut out to be his temporary guardian.

Right now she feels a failure. Not just regarding Jack but managing the farm. She's in debt, she's tired, the farm ought to be producing more, she hasn't the time to be making the cheeses or the butter which should command a better profit, she can't think clearly enough to make proper plans for the future. She's afraid of making friends and knows that locals are still slightly suspicious of her. It feels like she is swimming against the tide with her head barely above the waves.

Goodness knows what has happened to the RAF station and the masts after yesterday's bombardment. It must be of real importance to the Germans to target it twice in the space of a few days.

She wonders how much Arthur knew and what drove him to do what he did. Whatever's going on up there on the downs has surely had a drastic set-back and what of the personnel working there? There were plenty of ambulances and other emergency vehicles in attendance. Did Arthur actually have a hand in bringing this about, she wonders. It makes her sick to think so. In hindsight she realises how naive she was. How little she knew of her own husband. She had been harbouring a few suspicions about him for a little while, but it wasn't until an evening back in early March that she started to seriously consider the thoughts that were bothering her.

It was a typical sort of evening, nothing particularly unusual. She watered the seedlings on the kitchen windowsill then sat down for the first time that day. She rubbed her eyes. There always seemed to be one more thing, or two or three, to do every evening before she could stop and relax. The only way to stop some days was actually to go to bed and she would have done that half an hour ago except Arthur was still out. Not that she needed to stay up for him but she tried not to cause anything that made difficulties in their relationship. He was quick to jump off the deep end at her if she said things that displeased him. It was easier in the long run to tow the line whenever she could, but she still managed to regularly say things that she thought were quite innocuous but for some reason set him off on a rant.

This evening he told her he was going to the Crab and Lobster but she had begun to wonder if he was seeing a mistress rather than frequenting the pub. He'd been out quite often lately of an evening, more than he used to. She examined her own feelings about this possibility and realised she was not particularly jealous, more annoyed that he left her to finish all the chores while he went out enjoying himself. Should she voice her suspicions she wondered, or just wait to see how things turned out. Best to wait, she thought. However, she was curious enough to wonder who the unlucky lady might be.

Neither she nor Arthur had had the energy or the inclination for sexual relations for quite some time and she wondered if another lover was Arthur's reason - or maybe it was the reason he had a lover in the first place. It certainly wasn't hers. Taking a lover couldn't be further from her thoughts. She was just too dog tired at night and didn't particularly enjoy sex anyway.

Never had done. And where would she have the opportunity if she wanted it? She didn't socialise in the pub or attend Young Farmers meetings. There was never enough free time for that even if she wanted.

In the end she took herself to bed but heard him come home not long afterwards and creep into bed beside her smelling of tobacco.

In the morning at breakfast he announced, 'I'm thinking of buying Bob Taylor's Triumph off him.'

Elsie was surprised to hear this coming from a man known for his miserly attitude towards spending money. Not that they ever seemed to have much spare to splash out.

'Taylor's motorcycle? Bit pricey for us isn't it?'

'Bout time we modernised. It'll make life easier fetching the pig swill and carting feed sacks back from the store'.

His logic was sound. It would certainly be quicker than harnessing up one of the horses every time but Elsie thought he would probably change his mind once he'd looked into it and found out how much he'd have to part with.

'Can you ride a motorcycle?' She asked him.

'Course. Anyone can ride a motorcycle, even you! Bob's got a trailer to go with it too.'

It was a few days later that she found she had underestimated him. He told her in the morning he was going into town for supplies and at midday she heard him puttering up the track on a new motorcycle and trailer which he proudly parked in the yard, looking like a cat with new whiskers.

'Arthur! How can we afford something like this?' It was a decent looking motor and must have set Bob Taylor back a tidy penny.

'Stop worrying woman! It's all paid for.'

It wasn't like Arthur to splash out on something without weeks of mulling it over and trying to find a cheaper version of whatever it was he was after, and especially paying the price all in one go. She felt suspicious of this latest splurge. She could tell that any more enquiries from her would set him off on one of his rants so she kept her counsel, but he was certainly acting in a dubious manner recently.

The next day, being a Tuesday evening, Arthur did his usual twice-weekly round, delivering milk and cheese to the RAF station and bringing back the last three days of pig swill. This time, instead of the time consuming task of harnessing up the horse he hitched the cart to the motorcycle, loaded the empty swill pails, the milk churn and cheese, revved the engine of the Triumph with a roar and squealed off with reckless speed out of the yard and up to the station, minus any MOT and insurance.

A few days later, while Elsie was busy in the dairy, she happened to glance out the window to see Arthur's mate, Billy Price, walking across the yard. She opened the door and called out to him,

'Billy Price, are you looking for Arthur?'

'Eh, yes. I guess he's at the milking shed?'

'I think he's loading the muck cart.'

'I'll go on up.'

Billy didn't say why he'd come.

Later she said to Arthur, 'I saw Billy earlier, what did he want?'

'Oh, nothing much. He was just passing.'

Just passing? Elsie was not completely naive. She knew when someone was being evasive so she could tell Arthur had something to hide. She suspected it may have something to do with another liaison with a lover. She did not pry.

What Arthur had to hide was far more sinister than an extra marital affair.

CHAPTER 9

PIECES OF BAD NEWS

With a start Elsie realises the time and she's still in her old grey dressing gown and the cows will be waiting at the gate soon. She hurriedly washes and heads out to start the day's work.

After milking she brings the pail of milk and puts a jug on the table before walking down to the post box. Two letters today. The brown one is likely another bill that she doesn't even want to look at. The white one is postmarked from Clacton on Sea addressed to Jack Patton. Could it be from the mother, she wonders.

Returning to the kitchen, Helen has the porridge ready - a welcome development that Helen seems to have taken upon herself.

Fortunately the lad doesn't appear to have any lasting effects after his ordeal yesterday, except perhaps a little quiet.

'A letter for you, Jack.' She tells him.

He looks at it for a moment in surprise, before tearing the envelope.

'It's from Mum,' he says looking at Helen.

Helen looks over his shoulder. 'Shall I help you read it?'

He nods and she crouches by his side taking the single sheet of paper, scanning it quickly and raising her eyebrows in Elsie's direction.

She reads out loud.

Dear Jack.

Hello son, I hope you're enjoying yourself on the Isle of Wight. I hope you're being good and remembering to be polite and helpful. Have you made lots of friends down there?

Well I have some news. I've given up the house on the estate and Bert and I have moved into a holiday chalet at Jaywick, near Clacton, that belongs to Bert's uncle. It's quite near the sea and much safer from the bombing than being in London. The estate has mostly escaped the bombs so far but night after night we heard the planes and the explosions. I'm doing some cleaning jobs here and Bert's working in a factory so we are doing alright. It's only a small place so you'll be better off staying where you are for now till the end of the war. I'd come and see you if I could but it's a long way to the Isle of Wight and we can't afford it at the moment.

Your cousin Babs has left London too. They've gone up to Yorkshire. Aunty Evelyn sends her love.

Try to write something to me, Jack. The address is at the top of the page.

Regards to the people looking after you.

Love, Mum and Bert.

'When is the war going to be over?' he asks.

Helen tries to reassure him. 'Well, we don't really know at the moment, Jack, but hopefully it won't be too long.'

The lad sits and stares at the letter.

Elsie suggests that Helen helps him write a letter back to tell his Mum all about the farm and what he's been doing.

Jack shakes his head and runs upstairs.

Jack

I crawl under the bedclothes with Oscar. Why has she gone to Clacton, I silently ask him. Oscar wipes away some tears that suddenly appear. I feel angry and jealous. Bert gets to live with Mum and I'm sent away here. I thought I was sent here to be away from the bombs but there's more here than on the estate. I don't know where Clacton is except near the sea somewhere. Perhaps Bert likes fishing. I'd like to go fishing. Not with him, though. I ask Oscar when I'll be able to go to Clacton but he waggles his woolly ears telling me he doesn't know. It depends when this Mr Hitler stops sending bombers over here.

Aunty Helen comes into my room and sits on the bed beside me. I stay under the covers and shut my eyes. I don't want to talk to her, but I don't want her to leave either.

'I know how disappointed you must be feeling, Jack, but while you're staying here on the farm, there's lots of new and interesting things we can do together. Don't forget Mrs Dyer promised to show us how to milk a cow on Sunday. That's going to be fun, isn't it?'

I manage to nod. I don't want her to see I've been crying.

'Well,' she says, 'I have to go and visit my husband this afternoon, so when you're ready, why don't you come down and we can spend another hour getting the garden straight before I leave.'

I nod again, she pats me and goes downstairs.

I like her. She's kind to me.

Helen.

I enjoy a leisurely stroll down to the hospital, enjoying the warm summer weather. I wear my sunglasses and my red polka dot dress. The trees along the Undercliff are full of birds, chirping and singing and the sea sparkles through the gaps in the leaves. It's difficult to think, on an afternoon like this, that bombs were raining down on us yesterday.

Jack shows real interest in how vegetables that he has seen in the greengrocer actually grow in real life. It's easy to forget that children from cities don't have the opportunity to experience the countryside, or even simple gardens sometimes.

I enjoy pointing out insects we unearth or butterflies keeping us company so that he doesn't become fed up with the actual weeding and hoeing. He's careful to gently move any earthworms out of the way of the trowel and is less squeamish about them wriggling over his palm than I am.

He was quite upset about the letter this morning but never says much about his mother. It's difficult to guess what's going on in his head. I was tempted to raise the subject while we were in the garden but thought perhaps it was still too raw with him. I'll see if he will talk about his home life over tea tonight, although he is still clearly in awe of Mrs Dyer. As I am, I suppose!

I reach the hospital and look in wonder again at the marvellous Victorian facade which is so long I can barely see the last section of the building.

As I approach Gerald's room nurse Page, who is the one responsible for Gerald's daily care, leads me to one side.

'Mrs Day, your husband had a very bad night, struggling to breathe and coughing blood. The consultant was called this morning and Mr Day was taken for X-ray. I'm afraid his right lung is still badly infected and has deteriorated. The consultant considers the best course of action is an artificial pneumothorax intervention, surgery to collapse the lung', she adds, seeing my incomprehension. 'It allows the lung to relax and heal. For the rest of the day he is on complete bed rest and scheduled for surgery on Monday afternoon.'

I am stunned. Gerald seemed so much better yesterday until that awful coughing fit.

'Am I allowed to see him?'

'Half an hour, Mrs Day. Don't let him get agitated.'

Gerald is flat on his back with his eyes closed. I sit down and take his hand.

He squeezes it back. 'Rum do, isn't it?' He mutters.

I try to reassure him that it's just a set-back and he's strong and resilient so we'll get through it. It's reassurance for myself as much as for him. I hadn't expected a relapse such as this and realise I need to double my efforts to obtain more work as the costs are likely to rise.

Gerald obviously finds it hard to appear cheerful this afternoon, but to give him his due, he tries. I leave him after 30 minutes, eyes closed and shut into his thoughts. It's too much effort to talk.

Feeling low and deflated with this set-back I find the footpath leading towards the sea and follow the cliff path into town trying to clear my thoughts and telling myself not to worry. The sea is gentle today in a range of pastel blues, greens and purples under an ultramarine sky dotted with the typical cotton wool clouds floating above me. The lazy white surf creates lace patterns on the shingle. The scene is immensely calming and by the time I reach the edge of town I feel more positive. Gerald will pull through this. It is just a minor set back.

I plan to call into the stationers to renew a card I put in the window advertising for work and also with a mind to purchase another comic for Jack to cheer him up after this morning's disappointment. While there I scan the shelves and see that they have a small selection of children's books. Instead of the comic I buy Fun on the Farm and John and Mary go to the Seaside. He won't be able to read them himself yet but I hope they will inspire him to learn if I offer to help, so it gives him a better start when he joins the local school.

I stroll past the recruiting office and look at the posters in the window. It crossed my mind a while back to volunteer for the forces but if I had a choice I'd prefer to do something less regimented. I must admit, though, the WRAF uniform looks very smart! There are quite a number of RAF and WRAF personnel in Ventnor, most are probably from the station near us.

There is a poster for the WLA, the women's land army and that looks a little more appealing, apart from the awful brown dungarees. I did hear, though, that the WLA recruits girls younger than the forces do and I have an impression of young, green teenagers straight out of college or little office jobs. Mrs Dyer's opinion also bears this out. I'm no doubt doing them a colossal injustice, but I can't picture myself being part of it. Besides, I'm already lodging on a farm, Mrs Dyer's labourers have left and she's considerably overworked, so perhaps I should look nearer home to do my bit.

When I arrive at the farm late afternoon no one is around the house so I take a walk outside. Mrs Dyer is at the milking but Jack isn't there. Eventually I find him in the kitchen garden picking tomatoes.

'Hello,' he says, looking more cheerful than this morning, 'Mrs Dyer told me to pick the marrow and anything else that was ready. We're having marrow for tea. Are these tomatoes red enough?'

I help him pick the last of the fruits and we walk back to the house companionably.

'Is it really a long way to Clacton from here?' he asks me.

So he might be more cheerful but his mother's letter is still preying on his mind.

'Yes Jack, it is quite far and it might be very expensive for your Mum to take a coach or train all that way. I'm sure your Mum would like to have some news from you, though, and I could help you to write something.'

He looks doubtful.

'Anyway,' I continue, 'I've got something for you today and I'll show you after tea.'

'What is it, what is it?'

'Small surprise for after tea, so you will have to be patient, and don't forget we are milking a cow tomorrow!'

He skips on ahead of me with two new things to look forward to.

On Sunday after a slice of bread and jam we don our boots and wander up to the milking shed to wait for Mrs Dyer and Mr Simmons to finish the milking.

A cow remains tethered in the shed awaiting our novice ministrations.

Mrs Dyer says, 'this one is Snowdrop. She's a very patient cow.'

She directs us to sit on one side of the cow, herself on the other on the small milking stools.

She holds a teat of the udder and explains how to squeeze each finger in turn in a rolling motion, moving down the teat. She demonstrates and the cow produces a satisfying squirt of milk. I have a turn with Mrs Dyer's guidance and manage to coax out a small dribble. With some perseverance the milk eventually hits the bucket with an acceptable splash.

When Jack has a go his little fingers are too small to produce any result, so Mrs Dyer places her hand over Jack's small fingers on another teat to help him to succeed. Instead of hitting the bucket the squirt of milk jets out sideways and hits Jack squarely on the nose. I start to giggle. Mrs Dyer tries not to laugh at first. Jack's expression of surprise changes to concern that he's done something wrong but eventually we are all three laughing as Jack wipes his face with his sleeve.

'We managed a good squirt there, Jack,' says Mrs Dyer, and it's so good to see her relaxed and happy for once. We continue with our lesson until poor, patient Snowdrop is milked and then make our way companionably back to the farmhouse for breakfast.

Afterwards, Mrs Dyer pushes the pile of papers further to the end of the table with a sigh. 'I just can't find the time to deal with all this and it seems to grow each day. My husband used to do it all. I will have to get to grips with it before the bailiffs start knocking.'

I can see that this is not an admission she is taking lightly. She is a proud woman who doesn't easily ask for help, so I seize my opportunity and tentatively approach the subject that has been worming its way through my mind. I make a suggestion.

'If it suited you, Mrs Dyer, I could deal with it for you as that's the sort of work I'm used to doing, and after all, it's also what I'm doing for Mr Taylor and Mr Timms at Wroxall.'

I suggest that I would be happy to consider a reduction in rent to compensate.

'I have plenty of time on my hands at the moment as I havent managed to secure a job yet, and would consider taking on some paid farm work as well.'

I'm surprisingly nervous approaching this with Mrs Dyer. I just can't anticipate what her reaction will be. I plod on regardless.

'I'm aware I have no experience although I'm sure I could do at least as well as any land girl. What do you think?'

She pulls the pile of paperwork back towards her and starts flicking through it while she ponders the suggestion. Eventually she nods.

'If you could deal with the accounts it would be a weight off my mind, I have to admit. I'll give some thought to the other.'

We agree on a rent discount and for me to work a morning each week on the paperwork and any other things that may crop up. I begin to feel more positive with three mornings work to keep me occupied. I have a feeling Mrs Dyer will eventually agree to me working on the farm. She seems to have a resistance against land girls but I think that now she knows me and I live here, she will see the sense of it.

While Mrs Dyer is at the milking shed the next morning, I sit at the kitchen table and pull the pile of papers to me. I retrieved her account book and another pile of unfiled papers from the bureau in the small area off the sitting room that's loosely described as the office. I prepare to sort out the urgent from the already dealt with and a quick look at the account book tells me that if it was her husband who kept the books he probably left in April as the handwriting changed then, although there are only a handful of entries since. The rest is obviously amongst this pile in front of me somewhere.

I make a separate pile of bank statements and cheque stubs and another of outstanding bills but delay their payments until I've ascertained how much Mrs Dyer has in the bank in order to pay them. The concentration on the job in hand is good for me today to keep my mind from dwelling on Gerald's looming operation. I was advised not to visit at all today but I will walk down to the telephone box late afternoon to see if there is any news.

By noon I sit back rubbing my temples. I have cross referenced the cheque book stubs and the paying in books with the account book and bank statements up to mid June but still need to work my way through the outstanding paperwork to determine what monies Mrs Dyer has to her name. Fortunately Jack has been occupied with his new books for much of the time and then went out to play somewhere as he could see I was engrossed in the work at hand.

Although we agreed on one morning a week, I really want to bring the account book up to date so that we can settle the urgent bills and I decide to spend at least a couple of hours on it the next day.

Jack

I had a ghastly shock this morning. When I went to the barn for the chicken's corn, I opened the door and there right in front of my face were two bloody rabbits strung up by their feet.

I jumped back with a scream, my heart pounding.

No one heard or came so I stood outside a while until I calmed down enough to creep back into the barn and edge round the rabbits to collect a bowl of corn. From a safe distance I looked more closely at the poor creatures with cloudy eyes and dark blood crusting around their mouths and noses, drying dark crimson almost black. There was a small pool of it in an old dish on the floor to catch the drips.

I wanted to tell Aunty Helen but she was working at the kitchen table again today and I knew I shouldn't disturb her so I went and sat on the tractor for a while, imagining I was a proper farmer with a field to plough. It wasn't much fun on my own, though, so as it was grey and very windy today I went back indoors and lay on my bed with Oscar and my new books. I wish I could read them myself but the pictures are good and Aunty Helen read the first few pages of the seaside story with me. I've never had a proper story book of my own. I usually get an annual for Christmas which I like, and then that starts me wondering if I will go home to my Mum at Christmas this year.

Clacton isn't home, though, so I can't even imagine it. Will my annuals and farmyard be there? Where will I sleep? I wish I had someone to play with today.

Later I hear Mrs Dyer come in and Aunty Helen calls me for lunch. It's bubble and squeak with a sausage meat rissole. Quite tasty.

'There's two dead rabbits hanging in the barn,' I blurt out, which, of course is a bit stupid of me because Mrs Dyer must know that.

'Yes,' she says. 'I shot them yesterday evening. Rabbit stew for tomorrow.'

I look at her in surprise. 'We're going to eat them?'

'Of course we're going to eat them. Free meat. Plenty more where they came from too.'

I concentrate on my bubble and squeak. I don't think I've ever eaten rabbit before because my Mum buys meat from the butcher. I hadn't thought about them being shot. I feel quite sad for the rabbits. There's more to being a farmer than I thought.

Later in the afternoon I go out to the yard to check if there are any more eggs and the feed barn door is open wide. Mrs Dyer stands there in the doorway with a log of wood in front of her and a dead rabbit spread across it. The other one is still hanging by its legs.

She has a knife in her bloody hands and there is a mess of innards which she scrapes into the dish on the floor. The smell is something awful and I want to run but somehow I stand rooted to the spot and have to watch in grim fascination. She turns towards me. 'If you want to be a farmer, Jack, you have to do things like this.'

I dare to take a step closer, wrinkling my nose. Mrs Dyer is just like a butcher. She chops off the poor rabbit's head and I nearly scream, and then she seems to pull off it's skin like she's taking a fur jacket off, leaving a skinny purple and cream carcass on the block which she hands to me.

'Take it into the scullery, Jack, and put it on the draining board, there's a good lad.'

I don't really want to touch it, but I can't exactly refuse without being called a ninny again so I take a deep breath and hold the slimy thing by its feet, thinking that I can see a slight smirk on

Mrs Dyer's face.

Helen

I hurry along the Underclifff Drive to the hospital on another damp and blustery day. It has become quite unseasonable for August these last few days and I've worn my light green water-proof coat in case it pours down later. I failed to glean much from the telephone call to the hospital yesterday except that Gerald was 'comfortable'.

I find him flat on his back in the bed again with his eyes closed and a tumbler of water on the side table with a bent straw in it.

I hold his hand. 'Hello my love, how are you feeling?'

'Uncomfortable', is his response.

His breathing is shallow but slow and he forces a smile. I suspect he is finding it difficult to keep up a conversation.

Nurse Page enters the room.

'Ah, Mrs Day. Your husband had a successful operation yesterday to collapse his right lung. He is back on complete bed rest for a while while his lung is given a chance to relax and heal itself. I expect he is still sore and best he doesn't talk too much.'

I tell her I understand and eventually after fussing with bed-clothes and offering Gerald a sip of water she leaves us in peace.

I sit beside the bed on the balcony and take it upon myself to chat about the everyday things of life here, what we've been doing on the farm, Jack's letter from his mother and my work sorting out Mrs Dyer's accounts. After an hour or so it is clear that my husband is drifting so I kiss him lightly and promise to visit again tomorrow.

CHAPTER 10

The man stood at the bottom of Bonchurch steps. It was always dark there at the best of times but then it was late evening on a damp March night in 1940 with no one around and a blackout in force. The man was of average height, wearing a thick black coat belted at the waist and a fedora pulled low over his eyes so that Arthur could not see his features.

'The plans?' The man held out a leather gloved hand.

Flicking a cigarette lighter briefly, he glanced at the papers that Arthur handed over and with a nod placed his other hand inside his coat and pulled out an envelope. Arthur looked inside and without counting it, placed the money in his inside pocket.

'I'll be in touch,' said the man and promptly turned his back and walked briskly in the direction of the town.

Arthur stayed where he was and, cupping his hand over the light, lit a cigarette, watching the man disappear into the night. He knew nothing about the man, no name, no occupation, just the time and location for the exchange.

He walked slowly back up the steps where Billy Price waited, smoking, at the top. Price looked inquiringly at Arthur who nodded and patted his breast pocket.

'He said he'd be in touch.'

Heads down, they walked together back up the hill.

CHAPTER 11

FIGHTING SPIRIT

Helen

For days we've had wave after wave of bombers coming over. The very sound of them worms it's way inside us, filling us with fear and dread. Our boys come flying over to meet them and we watch fearsome dog fights over the channel while holding our breaths whenever a plane comes spiralling out of the sky, smoke billowing and we look hopefully for a parachute, whoever it may be. We hear distant explosions echoing over the sea as the German bombers target the shipping convoys making their perilous way across the channel. The air raid siren wails out in annoying regularity. Sometimes we head for a shelter, but most times we take a leaf from Mrs Dyer's book and carry on regardless. When the planes are high they are mostly heading over to London which has been bombed relentlessly and we can hear the deep booms of the anti-aircraft guns trying to bring them down before they reach the mainland. There are just too many of them though. Germany appears to have an inexhaustible supply of bombers and each evening on the news we hear that another area of London has gone up in smoke. All those poor civilians, injured, dead, homeless, bereaved. The fighting spirit goes on, though. We won't let those Nazis grind us down. Every evening the three of us gather round the wireless in the sitting room and listen to Mr Churchill updating us on the war progress. He keeps our spirits up, no matter what. Most of us realise there must be many horrors of the war that we are not told about and perhaps that's best. A demoralised nation would be suicide.

This evening, after tea, Mrs Dyer goes out on the farm again to fill the water troughs and top up the hay. She takes a gun under her arm so I guess we'll be having rabbit stew again soon.

Jack and I wash the dishes and clear away, and finally I pump up a fresh jug of drinking water from the well in the yard before settling down with Jack to help with his reading. He's shown good progress in a few weeks.

Mrs Dyer joins us in time for the news. The news is sobering. Last night London was severely bombed for hours. The first time we've heard of a serious night raid and Mr Churchill ominously calls it the Battle of Britain. We sit for a moment thinking about all the poor unfortunate souls caught up in the disaster and think it was probably wise for Jack's mother to move to East Anglia. Jack, fortunately is too young to appreciate the enormity of it all and although he listens to the news and can see we are moved by it, he soon turns his attention back to his books.

We wrote a letter to his Mum last week. Jack wanted to tell her about the milking escapade and the jobs he's been doing to help on the farm. He didn't want me to write anything about the bombing - I don't know if that is good or bad. We haven't heard back from Mrs Patton yet.

CHAPTER 12

ARTHUR

Elsie has left Simmy mucking out the stable this morning while she cranks up the tractor and heads to the barn to collect straw bales to take up to him. After moving the bales she notices Arthur's motorbike where it's been left in the barn, gradually becoming hidden by straw and chicken droppings. She had forgotten it was there, covered with an old grey tarpaulin. He didn't have much use out of the machine after all, she muses. She now has a pretty good idea how he paid for it, but has not mentioned it to anyone. Best to keep quiet about that purchase, she thinks, especially as there's nothing in the accounts. She reflects back to the last evening she saw him drive the machine.

It was about seven thirty in the evening when Arthur left the kitchen, telling Elsie he was off to the RAF station with the swill bins. He attached the cart to the Triumph and loaded a hunk of cheese, a churn of milk and the empty swill bins. It was a lucrative contract with the RAF and the pig swill came free.

Kick-starting the Triumph, he counted his blessing for this new acquisition as it saved him bringing the horse up to the yard and fussing around harnessing her up. Always a time consuming business he had little patience for. Instead he just needed to jump on the motorcycle and away he could go. He supposed he ought to find some insurance but as the station was just along the way he hadn't bothered just yet.

'I'm meeting Billy Price for a swift half at the Crab and Lobster afterwards,' he told Elsie as he knew this particular errand may take him longer than his usual round.

The guards at the gate knew him by sight now and ushered him through with a few ribald comments about his fancy new motorcycle, which he waved away with a laugh and a V sign.

He pulled up at the canteen, tooting the horn to rouse the cook. A few WRAFs were standing outside smoking and a couple of men joined them before all wandering off without giving him much of a glance.

Alexei, with a surname Arthur couldn't pronounce, came out to greet him, wiping his hands down his greasy apron. Head cook, with a finger on the pulse of the station, and happy to gossip, especially if it meant a backhander for information, no questions asked. Arthur found him a useful ally and usually brought an extra bonus for his personal use - an extra chunk of cheese, a pat of butter, a jar of cream, a half dozen eggs...

Arthur had already managed to map the layout of the station over several visits, during dark evenings. Sometimes Alexei would accompany him for a casual stroll, smoking and talking, Arthur surreptitiously memorising buildings, doorways, distances and pathways, casually pumping Alexei for information. All useful stuff for enemy eyes, but he hadn't managed to work out how much was underground, where it was and what exactly was happening at the station. Alexei was as much in the dark as Arthur was on the last point. In fact it seemed likely that only the top brass knew the true purpose of the place. Everyone else had a vague idea it was some sort of radio station, or early warning system, which the six high masts confirmed, but nothing more concrete than that.

On a couple of occasions Arthur had sneaked up to the masts without Alexei, keeping to the darkest shadows and making a note of their positions. Alexei appeared to have pretty good knowledge of the layout of the place and with a certain amount of pumping and convivial sips from the whisky flask Arthur kept in his pocket, he began to build up a plan in his head of the underground bunkers where the main operations were carried out. On this occasion they took their usual 'casual' stroll around the site, ostensibly sharing a cigarette break, gradually gleaning the information Arthur needed. Before he took his leave, he discreetly passed over a couple of notes to the cook before he rode off with the pig swill.

Billy Price was sitting in a quiet corner of the Crab and Lobster nursing a pint. Arthur nodded to the publican for the same for him.

When Arthur sat down, ensuring they were not being overheard, he brought out a pencil and drew in a notebook the underground workings of the RAF station as best as he could work it out - information he had just gleaned from Alexei and their stroll around the buildings. They studied the new information and Billy agreed to take Arthur's notes and diagrams to draw out acceptable plans to pass to their contact. He took the notebook and tucked it into his inside pocket. Keeping up appearances, he stayed a while longer, talking about the war, the farm and Arthur's new motorcycle, before taking his leave.

'I think Elsie's getting suspicious of these late night escapades, Billy, but she won't have a clue what we're about.'

'Just as well I'm doing the drop this time, then, or you'd have another late night.'

With that, Arthur downed the last of his second pint and made his way home.

Elsie was slightly surprised when Arthur returned before ten. He wasn't even half-way drunk, either, although she guessed it was more than the 'swift half. It always was.

Today she eyes the redundant Triumph and wonders what she should do with it. Nothing at the moment, she thinks, as she's got more than enough on her plate. She swings the tractor out of the barn and heads up the track.

CHAPTER 13

WAR WEARS ON

Helen

I rub my eyes. It's been difficult to sleep through the nights this last week. For one thing it has been hot and humid and even with my window as wide as I can open it, I have lain with just a sheet over me, feeling restless. Then, come the darkest hours and I can hear the drone of planes in the distance and the deep boom boom of the anti-aircraft guns as wave after wave of bombers makes its sinister way to blitz London and the south coast ports. The news is terrible. Huge areas of the capital ablaze. Thousands being made homeless. People being buried under tons of rubble. Hospitals becoming overwhelmed with the casualties and food and essentials becoming scarce.

I feel guilty that my life at the moment is relatively untouched by the war and vow to make a decision on what to do. Mrs Dyer has not yet approached me about working here, so I might reconsider my options. A visit to the recruiting office seems the best place to start, although I will mention the subject once more to Mrs Dyer before I burn my boats.

My visits to Gerald are taking much of my time and our afternoons trying to chat about something new are becoming increasingly difficult as Gerald has little in the way of news to relate to me.

He is still on total bed rest but hopefully by next week he may be able to sit up in bed, although there will still be little happening in his daily life. I don't want to be disloyal but really I don't need to be visiting every day. When I find work I may have to visit in the evenings anyway. I fear it will be tricky to approach it with Gerald.

As it happens, Gerald spares me from the worry.

At the hospital I find him in a more relaxed mood than lately, lying in the bed on the balcony as usual.

'Hello, love. You look very pretty this afternoon,' he says cheerfully.

I kiss him and sit on the chair beside the bed.

'The doctor came to see me this morning and he's really pleased with my progress. He says I can sit up in bed tomorrow, so that's something to look forward to! I never thought I'd look forward to such a trivial thing!'

We chat about the hospital regime and then the weather - how hot it's been these last few days. I lean over the balcony and survey the scene below me. The hospital grounds are extensive. Plenty of trees form a ring around the market gardens below which are lush with neat rows of vegetables. Men are busy with their cultivating tasks, most of them patients at the tail end of their treatment and I look forward to the time that Gerald is one of them. They even have livestock here. I can see the pig pen and Gerald thinks there must be a few cows as they are given good fresh milk every day. It's certainly a remarkable place.

I tell Gerald that my administration jobs at the two farms are going well and how I've been taking care of Mrs Dyer's accounts once a week, but that I feel I should be doing something more useful.

'Well, it sounds like Mrs Dyer needs more help managing the farm. Why don't you give her a hand? That would be useful, wouldn't it? You tell me you're a dab hand at milking now,' he teases.

He sees my hesitation. 'Helen, you don't need to worry about me every day. I appreciate you visiting every afternoon, but really you do need to be doing other things. What do you think?'

I return to the farm feeling that I've been let off the hook. Perhaps my husband can read my mind now. That's a worrying thought! I told him I would talk about it with Mrs Dyer, not letting on that I had already spoken with her. With my three morning's work, we can manage the hospital bills and my rent, so it's not essential that I'm paid for anything else. However, I do need to feel as if I'm being more useful in some way for the war effort and if I work in any way towards food production I will be exempt from conscription when it comes.

After supper I ask Mrs Dyer if we can discuss her accounts and other ways in which I might help. She's a difficult woman to pin down but this evening she takes a huge sigh and nods as if she hasn't the strength to argue or find other more urgent tasks to do in order to avoid the conversation.

I've brought her accounts up to date, paid all the bills that I'm able to, although there are three still outstanding and waiting for more funds to arrive in her bank. If she has anything urgent to pay for, like bomb damage, or veterinary bills, she does not have the means to pay.

I break this news to her.

'No surprise there,' she says, as she slumps, defeated on the settee. 'I had a feeling it might be worse.'

'Perhaps we should focus on the things that are most profitable and if you can take more advantage of that. I'm still willing to help on the farm.'

'The cheese used to sell well but you can see for yourself I don't have the time now', she says. 'Piglets sell well too but I need to get the boar in soon for Flo. She's old enough now to breed. That costs money that I haven't got and I still have to pay the hire of the bull. It feels like I'm running just to stay still. I have to find the funds in advance all the time before I reap any benefit.'

'Is there anything you can sell for immediate cash? The cheeses that you have left in the dairy, perhaps?'

She wrinkles her face. 'I've been hoping to keep those.'

She draws her lips into a tight line. 'I know what I have got, though. I could sell the Triumph. Surely that will pay for hiring a boar for my sow. Might even pay for the bull.'

'The Triumph?'

'Arthur's motorbike. He won't be needing that where he's gone.'

She spits out the last sentence with disgust.

I hadn't realised there was a motorbike on the farm but I see an opportunity to ask her about her husband.

'Mrs Dyer, where is your husband?'

She looks down, lips pursed. I wait.

'I suppose I might as well tell you. I'm surprised you haven't already heard from the town gossipers.'

She pauses a moment and looks at me directly.

'He's in prison. Let's leave it at that.'

September comes in warm and dry. Life on a farm never stays still and each season has its own tasks. I learn something new every day and it somehow feels very homely to be here, even though the work is tough.

After our uneasy start, the three of us have grown into a comfortable relationship with each other. Since Mrs Dyer confided about her husband to me, she seems a little less guarded. She has shed some of her reserve and softened the sharp edges of her nature a little and Jack has become more confident around her because of that.

He treats the farm just like his home now, spending his days in the open air helping to feed and water the livestock, riding on the tractor, and helping with other jobs as they come along.

As for me, my skin is tanned, my hair tied scruffily in a scarf, sleeves rolled up and a pair of dungarees purchased. Every afternoon now finds me perching on a milking stool helping Mrs Dyer and George Bailey in the milking shed. I'm becoming quite a dab hand at squeezing a teat! There's also something very special about milking that calms the soul. The soft breath of the cows, the warmth of their flanks where I rest my forehead, their soft munching of the hay, the delicious smell of the hay itself and the rhythmic splash of milk in the bucket. We become absorbed with the task in hand, lost in our thoughts and speaking little.

Mr Bailey is a pleasant old gentleman, a jobbing farm labourer all his life and now well into his seventies. A short, wiry man with grey whiskers and always sporting a well-handled cap. He turns up on his old bicycle in time for milking each day, says little, out-performs even Mrs Dyer in the speed of milking, cleans and sterilises all the pails in the dairy sink and leaves with a flourish of his greasy cap before clipping on his bicycle clips and cycling back home.

In contrast to the milking, the potato harvest was anything but calming. It was all hands to the work, including a number of teenagers from the town, earning pocket money that Mrs Dyer could ill afford to give. Backbreaking and heavy work pulling up the tubers, filling the sacks that Jack placed at the end of each row. Finally wheeling all the sacks out to the drive ready for the potato lorry. Fortunately for us, the weather stayed dry and mild. I can imagine on a wet and chilly day it would be a real slog.

We eat well and sleep well. Sometimes I guiltily forget for a moment that we are in the middle of a war. The effects on our lives are so little compared with the millions whose lives have been turned upside down. Of course we have daily reminders like the endless bombers flying over, the dog-fights over the channel, the shopping queues, the shortages and the annoying sirens. Every evening we have the somber news of the awful continuing blitz of London and other major cities, an update of Hitler's relentless march through Europe and the progress of our valiant troops fighting abroad. It all seems slightly removed from our uncomplicated rural lives here.

Jack is due to start school next week. He's quite excited as he will be with some of his friends again, including Jimmy who he has played with fairly regularly over the holiday.

Together we wrote to his mother again, even though there has been no other letter from her. I enclosed a note on behalf of Mrs Dyer to ask his mother if Jack had any other school clothes she could send, or if not, could she send some money so we can buy a new pair of shorts and a shirt. Having worn his school clothes around the farm for a few weeks before we managed to acquire some summer wear from the WVS shop, they look quite worse for wear. To date there has been no reply which is quite disappointing. It feels like it's a case of 'out of sight, out of mind' as far as her son is concerned.

I've grown very fond of the lad - I guess he has sparked my maternal instincts although I'm beginning to wonder whether Gerald and I will eventually have children or not. I like the way Jack holds my hand when we walk into town together and how he's happy to snuggle up to me when I read him a story or help with his own reading.

He has a typical boy's sense of humour. He put a worm in my gardening glove the other day and nearly fell over backwards with laughter when I shrieked and threw the glove onto the compost heap. I will have to watch him!

Gerald continues to make slow progress. I visit three or four times a week, usually straight after tea which I think is easier for both of us.

He has now been placed in phase two of the regime which means he can sit up in bed for short periods, while he waits for his rested lung to be reinflated the day after tomorrow. The doctor is pleased with his progress, although I know it seems to Gerald that he's hardly made any progress at all. At least at the moment he can read, eat normally and drink without a straw.

To relieve his boredom I suggested one day that he could write some short stories about the interesting or funny escapades he has encountered as a veterinary. To my surprise he has taken to the task with gusto and said he might put them all into a book one day. It's good to find something to take his mind off the tedium of his days. He will have to endure another few days being flat on his back after the operation, but hopefully it won't be too long before he can vacate the bed and sit in a chair sometimes. His legs must be so weak by now.

Jack.

I wake up today and by the time I go to bed I'll be six. I don't know if today will feel any different from usual. Mum used to give me a present at breakfast time. I had sweets last year and the model turkey for my farm. My Aunty Evelyn sent a card with a ten shilling note in, which is the most I've ever had. I bought a pencil case and coloured crayons with some of it, but I put the rest in my piggy bank.

Aunty Helen and Mrs Dyer both know it's my birthday because they made comments about me nearly being six.
'Wakey wakey, birthday boy!' Aunty Helen comes into my room to fetch me and she gives me a big hug. When I reach the kitchen, Mrs Dyer wishes me a happy birthday too, and on the table I can see two wrapped presents and a brown parcel.
We sit down for our porridge and afterwards I get to open the presents. There's one from Mrs Dyer and it's a small red tractor, just like hers. I'm so happy I jump up and down and I think she's pleased that I'm so happy because she laughs with Aunty Helen. My next present, from Aunty, is a pack of cards to play Snap and a blue and red yo-yo. I wanted one of those because lots of the boys at school play them in the playground and now everyone wants a go. I don't think Jimmy even has one yet.
'This parcel is from your Mum, I think', Mrs Dyer says, pushing the parcel to me. I can already see what it is from the shape. It's my usual tin of toffees and she's put a card with it and two half crowns inside, so that's nice. It feels quite special today, having a birthday, but I have to hurry up and get ready because I started the Ventnor school this week.
I feel very grown up when I walk down the street with Aunty Helen. I walk down the steps on my own and Jimmy and the two

Price brothers meet me at the bottom. Laurie and Don both go to the Primary school but Jimmy and I still have another year in the infants. The teacher, Miss Evans, is nice but very strict. I quite like being at school, but I miss being out on the farm all day. At least at school I can play with my friends more and we're allowed to take a book home from the classroom library each week.

I have school dinners with most of my class, although Jimmy goes home to have his. The dinners aren't very nice but I eat them. We usually get something like a Spam fritter with lumpy mashed potato and cabbage. Sometimes it's stew but it's always quite watery and not nearly as good as Mrs Dyer's and I wish they didn't keep giving us frog's spawn for pudding. It's disgusting. At playtime we get milk to drink which comes on a lorry in the morning. It's not such creamy milk as the farm milk, though. The week before I started at school I had a parcel from Mum. She sent a pair of my grey shorts and a shirt that she said she'd turn the collar on because it was all frayed. It's still the same, though, and too small for me now anyway. The two I brought with me are better. She sent two tubes of Spangles and a letter too.

Dear Jack,

I'm glad you are enjoying yourself on the farm. Milking a cow sounded like fun and I expect you're getting very big and strong with all that work outside. I'm glad you're making yourself useful. I'm sending you a couple of things for school as your landlady suggested and hope you are settling into your new class.

Bert and I are managing here in the holiday chalet but I don't know what it will be like in the winter. Probably cold and damp. Still, it's better than being bombed in London and you are in the best place. I had a letter from Mrs Grimes (the lady that I worked with who lived opposite your school) and she said some bombs fell on the estate a little while ago and a whole row of houses near the recreation ground were flattened. The doctor's surgery had a hit too so they've set up a temporary clinic in the community hall.

Money is a bit tight but I'll send you something nice for your birthday.
Enjoy yourself down there and be a good boy.

Love Mum and Bert.

I wonder if our old house is still standing and if we will live there again one day. The place Mum and Bert are staying in doesn't sound very nice. I'm glad I'm living in the Isle of Wight now but I hope they don't send any more bombs here. I've never been so scared.

Mum didn't mention me going to Clacton for Christmas like I thought I would, but I don't think I'd want to go there now anyway, especially as Bert is there all the time. I hope I can stay with Aunty Helen on the farm.

I've got lots of things to do here now. I carry fresh hay for the horses sometimes and I helped everyone on the potato harvest which was hard work running around with new sacks where they were needed and helping to collect the potatoes.

At school today, Miss Evans calls me out to the front of the class and she pins a cardboard badge on my jumper that has the number six. The class sing Happy Birthday to me, which is a bit embarrassing, but it's nice to feel special, as well.

Aunty Helen meets me at the top of the steps on my way back after school and when I come into the kitchen Mrs Dyer is there and she pours me a glass of milk then goes to the pantry and brings out a cake with six candles in. I'm so happy and I blow them all out with one puff.

'Make a wish, Jack,' Aunty Helen tells me, and I wish that I can stay on the farm during the Christmas holidays.

Today, on the way to school, I said to Aunty Helen, 'Is Mr Dyer a soldier, gone to war?'

'What makes you say that?' She asked me.

'I wondered if he might be coming home at Christmastime'

I've been wondering about him for a while and if he was likely to turn up at the farm one day, and if he turned up at Christmas he might not like me being there as well.

'No, don't you worry about that,' she said. 'He won't be home for a long time. He's away somewhere. Something secret, I think, to do with the war.'

I'm happy about that.

CHAPTER 14

INSPECTORS

Elsie

Elsie is in a fluster. She has just returned from the milking shed, more than ready for her porridge when two official looking men arrive by car in the yard. One man is from the Ministry of Agriculture, the other from the local agricultural committee. Gum booted and overalled they ask Elsie to accompany them on a round of the farm in order to complete a routine inspection on behalf of the Ministry.

'The Ministry requires all farms to make efforts to improve their production for the war effort, Mrs Dyer.' The more senior of the two inspectors informs Elsie. Nevertheless, it makes her nervous.

Simmy comes past wheeling the milk churns out to the farm gate and the ministry men stop to watch.

'How many gallons are you producing a day?' they ask. 'What's the size of your herd. What is the acreage of the farm?'

So many questions as they start to walk alongside her, back up the track to the milking shed.

They inspect the shed, asking who does the milking, checking her hygiene standards and the equipment.

'Have you considered one of the new vacuum milking machines?' they ask.

'It would speed up your production considerably, allowing you to increase your herd.'

Don't they live in the real world, she wonders. How does a single woman farmer afford a milking machine in these constrained times? She politely tells them that a machine will be too expensive for her at the moment, and that it's been necessary for her to half the herd size since her husband left. She hopes they don't follow that by prying over the whereabouts of her husband. However she notices 'a look' pass between them, so guesses they already have some indication.

The committee man says that if she increases her production of other necessities, she may be able to afford a milking machine.

'It would benefit you in the long run,' he adds.

Elsie buttons her lip. As they continue on their round she waits for any pearls of wisdom he may have for the suggested increased production.

'Are you growing potatoes?' they ask.

'Yes, we had a field of earlies and harvested a field of lates last month'.

There's nods of approval.

'What about feedstuffs. What do you buy in?'

Elsie knows that this is an area where she is likely to be criticised. She buys food for the pigs as she can never produce enough scraps now that the collection of swill bins from the RAF station have stopped. They used to have the whey from the cheesemaking too. Then there's cattle cake to supplement the hay she produces, as well as corn for chickens. She's well aware that farmers are being urged to be self-sufficient in livestock feed. Silage is the thing.

Sure enough, the two Ministry men confront her on this.

Elsie explains that 'for reasons beyond her control' she is unable now to collect pig swill from the local RAF.

'Well where do they send it now?' they ask her. She doesn't know.

They suggest she makes enquiries to resume her supplies.

That may be tricky, she thinks, but keeps silent on the subject.

'I noticed you have a silo,' the Ministry inspector observes, having spied the circular corrugated iron silo at the back of the hay barn as he went past.

Elsie admits she hasn't had time to make silage this year, with all her labourers gone to war.

They complete their circuit of the farm stopping to look at the fields, the cows and pigs.

Back in the yard they look in the hay barn and the stable, lifting the lids of the feed bins, and glance in the machinery and cart store.

'Is this a dairy?' they ask as they return to the yard.

Elsie explains that she's had to bring the cheese-making to an end and hopes they don't require a look inside. She doesn't want them to see how many cheese rounds she still has on the drying rack. She wants to keep them for home consumption rather than resort to the bland and paltry cheese ration on offer at the moment. And who knows how long the war will drag on, she thinks.

The committee man reassures her, 'We're not encouraging cheesemaking on farms at the moment. We need to save on our imports of bulky goods such as grain and feedstuff. They take too much room on valuable ships. That's what we need our farmers to concentrate on, as well as the staples like potatoes and milk.'

The other man takes the notebook and reviews what has been written.

'There are quite a number of improvements you could make next year. You have too many fields, Mrs Dyer, for the head of cattle you keep. You must bring more into production before next season. Is there anything we haven't seen yet?'

She takes them quickly to look at the kitchen garden and the small orchard. At least the garden looks in better shape than it had done a while ago and the apple and pear trees are still bearing fruit.

They walk back to the car.

'Well, as I said, you could bring your herd up to size if you purchase a milking machine. Otherwise you must plant up some of the fields for food or fodder, preferably both. I guess wheat will not be viable up here, but you could certainly increase potato production. I suggest a field or two of kale for silage and maybe turnips too.'

Elsie nods her agreement, her heart sinking.

The younger man chips in, 'I notice the ground in your orchard is just left to rough grass. This is a waste. You can plant potatoes between the trees, or even some of the fodder crops.'

'Also, if you revive the collection of pig swill, or find an alternative source, you can fit another two pigs in that field of theirs, as long as they are productive sows.'

Again Elsie nods her agreement, wishing they would hurry up and leave.

'You could join the land girl scheme for some extra help, you know. That may be the answer to your problems.'

'I've certainly been thinking about that. I can manage over the winter but may consider it in the new year,' Elsie lies.

They nod their approval, thank her for showing them around and tell her that she will receive their report and recommendations in due course.

She watches them drive off with relief but with a sinking feeling in her stomach.

Helen

October blusters in with rain, gales, fog and more rain. Almost every day, the same for two weeks now. Mud everywhere.

It's difficult to keep up the spirits in weather like this.

The fields are being churned to mud, especially round the gates where the cattle congregate. The pigs, of course, love it but the hens slink around in the barn looking fed up with it all and are not quite so willing to offer up the eggs. The cows are caked with mud, taking us ages to wash the udders before milking and the laundry hangs damp and limp over the clothes horse, blocking off the heat from the range.

The war grinds on with little in the way of good news. London continues to be blitzed, Coventry has been all but flattened,

Southampton and Portsmouth have received dreadful damage and so on. With awful regularity we see or hear the German planes going over, hear the anti aircraft guns and witness the aerial fights over the sea.

Daily we are being urged to 'tighten our belts', eat less, grow more, make do and mend, use less fuel and volunteer for the war effort. Many items have become scarce or non-existent in the shops, queues are longer and the black market is flourishing.

A few weeks ago, after the Ministry men came, Mrs Dyer became quite depressed. I found her one late afternoon sitting at the kitchen table with her head in her hands. I had just returned from collecting Jack from school and then fetching some errands from town, including some rat poison from the hardware store. It was a day of typical Ventnor mist which rolls in off the sea bringing drizzle and a chill to the bones even though the actual temperature is fairly mild for the time of year.

I shook the wet off my coat, kicked my boots off in the scullery and pushed the kettle onto the hot plate to make a pot of tea. I shooed Jack off to look for eggs.

Right then there was nothing I could say that would cheer up Mrs Dyer, so I quietly set the tea and sat opposite her and waited for her to talk if she wanted to. I knew she was barely managing and after receiving the report from the Ministry, I could imagine how overwhelmed she felt. Normally such a practical no-nonsense sort of woman, used to being in charge of things, this was a different side to her character.

'I don't know what to do, Helen,' she said, combing her fingers through her hair. 'Your help has been a godsend but there's so much to do to keep the Ministry off our backs.'

At that moment I could see from the account book that she was just breaking even.

Fortunately the Triumph was sold for a very satisfactory price which helped to clear her debts.

To start with we cleaned up the motorbike between us, oiled and greased it and wheeled it out to the end of the lane where we padlocked it to the lamp post, with a large for sale notice on it.

It was probably only a matter of time before some officer would tell us we were breaking a law but fortunately on the second day a young army corporal turned up wanting to buy it. Mrs Dyer quoted him a price that I thought was far too high, but he was prepared to pay it and went away a happy man.

'We need to make a plan,' I urged, going to the bureau in the office space and finding a pad and pencil. I brought her current account book too and the Ministry report.

'Let's look through the Ministry's report first. The milking machine. How much do they actually cost and how much time would one really save? Do you know?'

'More money than I can afford, and actually with a small herd like mine, even if we double in size, I don't think it would make enough profit to warrant the cost.'

The report was quite proscriptive. If Mrs Dyer kept the herd at the present size, she should set aside 30 acres of reasonable pasture. The rest of the farm should be put to a specific acreage of potatoes and the rest of the land made over to fodder crops. The report listed the fodder crops recommended and suggested she grew rye grass or flax for silage along with the collection of greenstuff like nettles and turnip tops.

'They don't want much, do they?' she said sarcastically.

The Ministry also expected her to improve her kitchen garden, keep at least two more pigs and obtain a regular source of food waste to feed them. The report warned that animal feedstuff would become scarce within the next year.

'This all looks like a ton of work. I hardly know where to start.'

I was certain that once Mrs Dyer could see a way forward she would rise to the challenge and lead the way. That's the sort of person she is. As for me, I'm more of an organiser than a leader and I know nothing about growing crops.

She pulled a sheet of paper and pencil towards her and started to draw a map of the farm and the fields. She muttered to herself as she wrote notes and calculations at the side, scribbling out, starting again. I poured ourselves some tea.

She pondered while she sipped the tea.

'How long do you think you'll be able to work for me, do you think?'

That wasn't the question I was expecting and I wasn't sure how to answer it. It depended on Gerald.

'Well, I guess it will at least be until the spring,' I told her, although what we do when Gerald is well again, I don't know. I doubt he will be strong enough to take on a veterinary job unless he specialises in domestic pets which was the area of work he least liked.

At the moment Mrs Dyer and I have an arrangement whereby I continue with my two farm accounts jobs which provide me with a little income, I deal with her accounts, take care of Jack and work on the farm all other times except Sunday afternoons which, as well as a couple of evenings a week, I devote to Gerald. All this in exchange for full board and lodging at no cost. It suits us both.

After Jack had gone to bed that evening we continued our planning, or at least Mrs Dyer did the planning and I listened and made the odd suggestion. We went to bed late but we finally worked out how much we could achieve between us and Simmy, the things that had to be purchased before any return on the outlay and the times when more labour would be needed.

Mrs Dyer agreed to make an appointment at the bank to try and secure a loan. She also agreed to make a visit to the Agricultural committee to see if there was any help they could provide in the way of seeds, loans, grants or hire of machinery. No harm in asking. We planned out which fields would be best for cultivation, partly because they were more on the level than much of the farm, and partly for convenience of being nearer to the yard.

A task assigned to me was to visit any schools, convalescent or nursing homes that may be able to offer us a regular supply of kitchen waste for the pigs.

Since then Mrs Dyer has been on a mission. It's like she's had a new vision and renewed drive to make her farm productive. Her energy is contagious and I find myself taking a proprietary interest in the place as if I have shares in it.

After fruitless visits to two local schools and a retirement home begging for kitchen waste, all of which had prior contracts, I managed to secure collection from smaller outlets in the town like the bakery, the Rose and Crown and St Catherine's Children's Home, who used to put their waste out for collection by the pig club, but as they had let the school down a few times recently the school agreed that we could have the swill instead.

It's now my job, having learnt to drive the tractor, to collect the swill three times a week. I need to pluck up courage to drive the horse and cart because fuel is becoming in short supply and we shouldn't be using it unnecessarily for me to use the tractor when it may be more useful for farm duties.

I'm learning new skills that I never thought I would, and collecting smelly pig swill is certainly one of them.

Today we plough up the first of the fields on the plan. I need to watch and learn as I will be thrown in the deep end before I know it.

Simmy and Mrs Dyer bring the horses down to the stable and I'm instructed as they harness the pair. At the field they are shackled to the plough and the day begins. To me the conditions don't look ideal after the heavy rain we've had. Our gumboots are caked and heavy and Simmy has to work hard to keep the plough cutting through on straight furrows. Fortunately up here the ground drains fairly quickly so there is no standing water and although claggy, the field doesn't become a quagmire. Nevertheless, by lunchtime all three of us have mud spattered up to our waists and we gratefully stop for Mrs Dyer's rabbit stew, nicely cooking in the range all morning. Even Simmy stays for lunch today so that we can use all the daylight for the task in hand. It's tough work and this is just the first field! Still, we have all winter to complete.

Elsie

Elsie walks briskly up the track in the pre-dawn half light, blowing on her hands in this chilly late October morning. The first frosty one, with a hint of wraith-like mist curling over the fields. The air is still, the mud on the track firm and sparkling, standing stiffly in rutted patterns. She loves mornings like this, crisp and fresh with a hint of pink brushing the edges of the mackerel clouds appearing out of the dark sky. Her breath clouds out in front of her as she calls to her cows, 'Come on girls,' although she has no need to call because they are all waiting around the gate, creatures of habit and eager to be milked, their combined breaths forming a misty cloud around their heads.

She sends them ambling their way down to the milking shed and closes the gate. She has kept the herd in these topmost fields these last few weeks. They are the most efficiently drained and least likely to become boggy. Unfortunately she'll have to bring the cows into the barn soon for the winter. The nearer fields aren't suitable for winter grazing. She trudges after the herd, opening the gate to the last available field as she passes. Although slightly daunted about the work ahead of them, and the costs involved, she is feeling strangely optimistic and less overwhelmed.

Back in July she had reluctantly advertised for a lodger as a last resort, but she is pleased to have Helen here. She hadn't realised that she missed someone to talk to other than Simmy and George.

Helen understandably asked the whereabouts of Arthur not long ago, but Elsie is thankful she hasn't pried any further into her affairs and neither has she been judgemental about Elsie having a husband in prison, unlike one or two of those gossiping crows in town, she thinks.

Elsie, somewhat reluctantly, but realising the necessity, made an appointment with her bank manager. After outlining their plan of action she came away with a substantial overdraft limit which she has already dipped into. Soon afterwards she took Simmy with her to the market and purchased two seven month sows which she has arranged to take to the boar this week. Hopefully piglets by early March. Her other sows should have piglets by Christmas. She can see their work being cut out, but at least they have a regular supply of pig swill again.

A further visit to the local Agriculture Committee to make herself known and she has signed up to a discount scheme for purchasing her seed potatoes and other bulk seeds depending on what she decides. She realises she just needed a prompt from someone to galvanise her.

It's been tough work but between the three of them they are slowly ploughing up the near fields. Although she has a tractor, it eats up precious fuel and is not really man enough for that particular job.

She's impressed how Helen has thrown herself into the work, although she still seems too timid around the horses and she should really get herself confident to take the horse and cart into town. Elsie plans to remedy that today.

Helen

'Right, Helen, it's you and me on muck spreading this morning,' says Mrs Dyer after our breakfast.

Oh Joy! Music to my ears!

We tramp our way up to the horses' field in the chill air, our overcoats buttoned up high. Rattling a bucket of old carrots at the gateway and the two come trotting down from the top of the field as soon as they see we come bearing gifts. Mrs Dyer entices them to the field stable where she bridles Biddy and tells me to lead her back to the yard. Squaring my shoulders I pretend to myself I've done this a dozen times. Animals know when you're nervous, don't they? I make a great show of patting the great neck and murmuring pleasantries in her ears in an effort to win her approval.

We make it to the yard without me having my feet trodden on by those great hooves and I watch while Mrs Dyer fastens a complicated-looking harness on the horse. She seems to name every piece of this intricate affair and I guess I'm supposed to commit it to memory, but that's a hope too far. She tells me to lead Biddy round to the dung cart at the side of the milking yard and so far, so good, I manage to carry out those simple tasks, feeling dwarfed by the huge muscular presence at my side, with feet as large as dinner plates.

Biddy is attached to the cart and I must now sit on the cart holding the reins and steer this whole living machine back out to the track and up to the middle fields. With a huge heap of dung piled up at the back of me, this could go horribly wrong!

Biddy knows the routine but she doesn't know which field we're going in. I negotiate the track and pause us while I hop down to open the gate. I shake the reins to steer us in and all seems well until she stops abruptly half way through the gateway and, taken by surprise, I flip backwards off my seat, making a less than elegant landing on the heap. By the time I scramble unladylike back on my seat all I can hear is the rare sound of Mrs Dyer's laughter as she walks up behind us.

'Oh my God, Helen. I wish I'd had a camera!'

Well, at least I've brightened someone's morning! She explains that I'm about to demolish the gatepost if I carry on at this angle but Biddy already realises this.

Mrs Dyer helps to back the cart and horse and we approach at a more oblique angle, negotiating the gateway with clearance on each side.

For the next half hour we take turns driving the cart and pitching the dung over the field. Not an easy task trying to keep balance so I don't pitch myself over the side, or take another dive into the dung.

After another learning curve to return Biddy and the cart to the yard, unharness her and brush her down in the stable, we have no further mishaps and I lead the horse back to her field feeling as if we at least have a little mutual understanding. One nil to Biddy, though.

I smell as ripe as a cowshed for the rest of the morning before I return for lunch and wash as much of the smell off me as I can.

Needless to say, Mrs Dyer has great glee relating my mishap in a very creative manner to Jack at tea time who reenacts it several times on the hearth rug for my benefit.

The evenings are too dark now for me to visit Gerald, so I've had to take time out of Wednesday mornings instead, as well as my usual Sunday afternoon visit. He has continued to make good progress and I find him sitting up in the bed on the balcony, thick blanket around his shoulders and a wooly hat on. He greets me cheerfully.

'Good news! I can actually get out of bed and sit in the chair tomorrow. It feels marvelous to have two lungs working again.'

He breathes in deeply just to prove his point but that starts him coughing.

'Alright, not quite out of the woods yet,' he says wryly, resting back on the pillows.

'Well, you keep quiet then and I'll do all the talking. This will make you laugh, though, so don't start coughing again or you'll have nurse Page come running.'

I relate my plunge into the dung heap, which does provide him with some amusement, and I update him on all the farm affairs. He shares his notebook with me where he has written his short stories about life as a veterinary. His writing is really rather good and quite witty. I make a mental note to look out for a really smart notebook or journal that I can give him for Christmas. It's difficult to think of something useful for someone who is chair or bed-bound all day. Perhaps a good quality fountain pen to go with it too.

'I don't know if I shall ever be working as a veterinary again, Helen. The doctor warned me that my lungs could be more susceptible to infection than they once were and that I might find heavy exertion difficult for quite some time. Some of my farm work used to be pretty strenuous.'

'You don't need to worry about that just yet, Gerald. I'm sure there'll be lots of related jobs that you'll be well qualified to do. Don't forget there's a war on and so lots of vacancies are available for men not eligible for service. You could also be a writer!'

I leave him in good spirits and walk briskly back to the farm. I feel so much fitter than when I arrived in Ventnor. I never have to stop and catch my breath now on these regular hikes back up the steep hills to the farm, and the heavy outdoor manual work on the farm has made me strong and tanned. I think the sea air is good for me, too. No wonder the chest hospital is here.

When I return to the farm I change into my dungarees and wander up the track to see what we're doing today.

Simmy is on the tractor, ditch digging. He seems quite content with his morning's task. I shout over the noise of the tractor, 'Where's Mrs Dyer, Simmy?'

He jabs his thumb over his left shoulder. 'Pigs.'

I find her in the middle of the pig's field erecting wire mesh fences to divide the field in three. The two newest sows are in one section, Flo and Dotty each in another.

She raises her hand in acknowledgement.

'Thought we ought to separate this lot before the first piglets come next month. Simmy's going to build another pigsty in each.'

She nods her head in the direction of a pile of corrugated iron and wood. 'Unless you're any good at building pigsties?' she adds hopefully.

I give her a look that says 'no chance' and help her to finish the fences. They need to be fairly robust to keep piglets in, so we use a sledge hammer to bash in plenty of posts to keep it stable. We are expecting the first litter to come about Christmas time and this week Mrs Dyer will take the new sows to the boar at a nearby farm which means we can expect another litter in the spring. I never would have guessed I'd be into pig rearing now!

In the evening we all sit around the wireless as usual to update ourselves on the war progress. Both Mrs Dyer and I make use of the time either knitting or darning. Mrs Dyer unravelled one of her husband's old jumpers and is remaking it for Jack for Christmas. I'm knitting a pair of fingerless gloves for Gerald for when he's sitting on the cold balcony. Wearing full gloves makes it difficult for him to write or turn book pages. I feel we are well into the 'make do and mend' for the war effort.

CHAPTER 15

CHRISTMAS

Jack

Today is the last day of term. It was really fun. No proper lessons to do and we had Christmas dinner and games in the afternoon. We've even come home early with our Christmas cards and snowmen that we made in class with toilet rolls and cotton wool. I will give mine to Aunty Helen.

I'm getting excited about Christmas although I don't really know why, but I'm glad I'm not going to Clacton, even though I suppose I'll miss Mum.

Some of my friends from London are going home for a few days. One of our old class teachers is taking them back, but we don't live in London anymore so I won't be going with them.

I hope Mr Hitler stops bombing at Christmas.

At the farm we made some paper chains out of old magazines and on Sunday we went for a walk over the downs and collected some holly and some bare branches which Aunty Helen painted with whitewash like snow. Mrs Dyer said she had some decorations in the loft and I think she is going to fetch them this evening. Our teacher said Santa Claus might not bring so many presents this year because of the war, but I don't usually get many presents anyway.

Last Christmas I had an annual from Mum and a tin of sweets. Sometimes I might get a game of some kind. My Aunty Evelyn brought me some things to put in my farm last year, but I don't suppose she'll send me anything from Yorkshire which I think is a long way away. On Christmas Day last year she and my cousin Babs came round in the afternoon. Babs and I played snap and Ludo, although she's two years older than me and cheated. Mum and Aunty Evelyn listened to the wireless and had a lot to drink. My Uncle Frank had already gone to war abroad somewhere and wasn't home for Christmas which Babs was quite upset about.

I don't know what it will be like being here with Mrs Dyer and Aunty Helen. I suppose it will be much the same as any other day because the animals will still need feeding. I won't even be able see Jimmy as he's going home with the others.

After sardines on toast for tea, Mrs Dyer brings the box of decorations that she fetched from the loft. There are mostly glass baubles, some of them very pretty, some painted wooden stars and some old paper chains that are all crumpled up.

'I think we'll bin these,' Mrs Dyer says, pulling out the paper chains and screwing them up.

Aunty Helen has put the whitewashed branches into a large pot and we hang the baubles all over it. It looks very festive. We pin up the paper chains that we made in the week, draping them across the room and now the sitting room looks like it's nearly Christmas.

I can smell something fruity and spicy coming from a pan on the range and when I ask, Mrs Dyer says she's making a special festive drink called punch, which is quite a funny name. I take the lid off and there's slices of apple floating on a red liquid. It smells gorgeous.

The morning of the day before Christmas is cold and still frosty when I venture out of the warm kitchen to fetch the feed. A little while ago Mrs Dyer cut down one of her husband's old woolen jackets and made it fit me. It's still very baggy but it's nice and warm. I also got a pair of long trousers from the WVS shop and I'm glad about that because my knees were getting chapped. My hands are chilly but I tuck them up into the over-long sleeves of the coat.

The sky is all stripey this morning with pink and gold and an orange sun is just poking up from the horizon. I stand and watch for several minutes until I can see the whole circle. It's really lovely. I never saw a sight like that in London.

I open the stable door to fetch some corn and there, hanging by its feet is a dead chicken. I'm getting used to seeing rabbits hanging bloody and cloudy-eyed before they turn up on the lunch table in the stew pot or a pie, but I haven't seen a dead chicken before. I enjoy the rabbit meals Mrs Dyer cooks, better than spam or rissoles, as long as I don't think about the dead rabbits too much.

'I see you've found Christmas dinner, Jack,' Mrs Dyer says as she comes across the yard ready to deal with it.

We haven't had chicken since I've been here, in fact I'm not sure if I've eaten it before. It's going to be something special. I can't remember what Mum and I had for Christmas dinner last year, probably sausages, but at least Bert didn't come round that day. If I stay and watch Mrs Dyer pluck and gut the chicken the smell alone might put me off my Christmas dinner so I leave her to the gruesome task and busy myself with feeding the hens and then the pigs to stay out of the way. When I arrive at the pig pen I have the second shock of the morning. I race back to the yard, yelling.

'Mrs Dyer, Mrs Dyer, Dotty has babies!'

She wipes her bloody hands on a rag.

'Marvellous, Jack. How many?'

'It looked like loads. Perhaps eight?'

We walk together back to the pig pen and she watches the new piglets sucking milk from Dotty.

'We'll have to watch out for Flo, Jack. She'll be next. Keep an eye out in case any of the piglets are getting squashed. These pigs can be a bit careless with their babies sometimes.'

The piglets are so tiny. All skinny, pink and hairless. They are very greedy too. I tip the pig swill into their troughs and wander back to the cow barn to top up the cow trough with their cake and mash. The cows are in for the winter now so we have to muck out the barn every day and put fresh straw for them.

There are a few cows that let me stroke their noses, blowing their warm breath at me but some are still quite nervous of getting too close.

I like being on the farm now and I still want to be a farmer one day. I think I'd like to have cows too. Maybe not pigs, but chickens are good and we'd want to have eggs. I think tractors could do all the heavy work so I wouldn't need to keep horses, and I'd be the one to drive the tractor. I don't think I'd grow potatoes.

I skip back to the yard to see what Aunty Helen's doing and I find her in the kitchen garden picking a swede and some leeks. There's not many left now.

Elsie.

Elsie allows herself an extra half hour enjoying the cosiness of the bedcovers before she has to brace herself for another frosty morning.

Christmas Day. It will be different this year with a child around, she reflects. In fact, different in several respects, not least the absence of Arthur which she guiltily feels relieved about.

The milk yield is tailing off now, as usual for this time of year and taking her less than half the time to milk the herd. With Helen's help she can afford to give Simmy the day off to spend with his wife and son's family.

This year she feels more enthusiastic to mark the day as more special than just an ordinary day. Joining in with Helen and Jack to make paper chains and decorate the house with greenery has been surprisingly enjoyable. Last evening they pinned one of Arthur's old boot socks beside the living room fireplace for Santa to deliver some treats for Jack, who carefully placed a mince pie and a carrot for Rudolph on a plate by the hearth. She must remember to remove it before Jack comes downstairs.

She's made a special effort with the Christmas dinner, with one of her plumpest chickens, chipolatas, herb stuffing, roast potatoes and vegetables from the garden. In lieu of the traditional pudding she has steamed a date pudding which she will serve with custard. It's been a pleasure to plan it all this year, unlike last year when she was full of anxiety and constantly on edge in case she caused a row when visitors were in the house.

Not that she had expected visitors.

Just two days before Christmas while she and Arthur were both in the yard, he said, 'I've invited Billy Price and his missus for Christmas Day.'

She gaped at him.

'Billy Price? But I've only got a rabbit in for us. That won't do for four of us.'

'Rabbit? We'll have a turkey. I've got it organised.'

'We can't afford turkey, Arthur. Why don't we kill one of the hens?'

'Stop mithering woman! I told you I have it organised.'

Her heart sank. She wasn't too keen on Billy Price. There was something sneaky about him that she couldn't really put a name to. She had only met his wife, Mary, a couple of times. She worked in an old people's home in Ventnor and Elsie thought her rather wet. She couldn't think of anything they would have in common to talk about over dinner.

She supposed that it would make a change from the last few years when Christmas Day was just a day like any others. In the first years she had made an effort to give Arthur a present and place a few decorations about the place, but she never received anything from him and he used to disappear down the pub for several hours, leaving her to try and keep the dinner hot way past the time he said he'd be home.

She gave up trying to make the day special after that. They didn't even go to church as neither were particularly religious, although she might have enjoyed the atmosphere once a year.

Although the day did turn out to be quite different from the usual, her misgivings were well placed.

Arthur brought her a large turkey - goodness knows where he had sourced it and how he paid for it - which she struggled to have ready in time in their unpredictable range oven. The roast potatoes were late to brown because the turkey was taking up too much room, and she finished up boiling all the vegetables for the same reason. She sweated all morning conjuring up a pudding that could be acceptable and hurriedly rustled up some mince pies.

The conversation was as strained as she expected although Arthur and Billy chatted amiably over their drinks to the exclusion of Mary and herself. By the time they left, late into the afternoon, Elsie felt exhausted but still washed the dishes and pans before hurrying to the milking shed to help with the last milk.

They ate turkey for the next week!

Hopefully, she thinks, this year will be less stressful with more enjoyable company. She looks forward to giving Jack his new warm jumper which she has spruced up with a bright blue stripe across the chest. It will make a pleasant change from his drab grey school jumpers. She purchased Helen a diary, produced by the local agricultural society which was on sale at the feed store when she last went, and she has added a new pair of stockings which she bought about three years ago when she thought she and Arthur were going to a harvest festival dance. Somehow they never went.

She finds Helen already in the kitchen with the tea made and the tell-tale mince pie and carrot whisked away. They walk companionably to the milking shed in the crisp dawn and Elsie reflects with a certain sadness that it may not be too many weeks before Helen leaves her. She will be visiting her husband this afternoon, who, she understands, is improving by the week. He is now able to make visits to the communal lounge, library and chapel, although it may be a little while before he starts gentle work in the grounds. Selfishly she hopes that his recovery is not too swift!

Jack

This is one of the best Christmases ever! Even Mrs Dyer was really nice to me and quite fun for a change. The knitting she had been doing in the evenings actually turned out to be for me and I wore my new jumper for the rest of the day. We had the best Christmas dinner I can remember and I had seconds of the date pudding too.

Aunty Helen had to visit her husband this afternoon and Mrs Dyer suggested taking her to the hospital in the horse and dog cart as it was a sunny day and we could go for a drive while Aunty Helen was visiting. It was brilliant. I had to wrap up warm as there was even some frost still around in the shady parts of the fields. We dropped Aunty Helen at the hospital which is absolutely massive, and then Mrs Dyer urged Biddy into a trot and we bounced along this tree-lined road called the Undercliff. Mrs Dyer said it was called that because of the high cliffs to our right. It was such fun. At a little village called Niton we turned around and trotted all the way back. Mrs Dyer said it did Biddy some good to stretch her legs otherwise she'd get too lazy.

We parked the horse and cart back at the hospital and we walked down the side of the hospital grounds and down some stone steps to a small bay called Steephill Cove. That's a good name for it because it was very steep to walk down! The wind was quite cold but the beach was lovely to walk on and as the tide was out, there were loads of rock pools to watch shrimps and crabs dashing about. It was the first time I'd been out any-where with Mrs Dyer but it felt alright as we climbed up from the bay and walked along the cliff path for awhile. She asked me about Mum and what we did for Christmas before I came here. I told her we didn't have such a good dinner as hers or crackers to pull and she seemed pleased that I'd told her that.

I wondered what sort of day they were all having in Clacton, but I think I'd rather be here.

Mum sent me a parcel with this year's Blackie's Childrens An-nual, a tin of toffees and a card wishing me happy Christmas. She added that she would write a letter soon, but I don't know why she didn't write it now and put it in the parcel. Aunty Helen told me I had to write a thank you letter tomorrow which is always difficult.

Aunty Helen gave me a box of dominoes and this evening Mrs Dyer plays a game with me and I win. Aunty also gave me some marbles but I'll wait for Jimmy to come back because he has some too. I also had a thick woolly hat in blue and black stripes with a bobble on top. It's much more fun and warm than my school cap for going outside to feed the animals. I curl up on the sofa and read my new annual from Mum, but Aunty Helen has to wake me up to go to bed.

Helen

A few days after Christmas dawns damp and misty but a degree or two warmer than lately, with no frost. Simmy has been given another day off as he worked on Boxing Day and Mrs Dyer and I can milk the cows between us now they are beginning to dry up. We sit companionably in the milking shed and Mrs Dyer asks me, 'how did you find your husband, yesterday, Helen?'

I tell her that I'm so pleased he's able to leave his room each day, now, and walk around the hospital. He's in much better spirits although still weak and in need of plenty of rest times, which the nurses make sure of. He lost weight while he was bed ridden but is slowly regaining it with all the good food he's given. Now he's champing at the bit to be allowed walks in the grounds.

'What will he do when he's finally discharged?'

'I don't know yet. He won't be able to manage a veterinary job, at least for a while, but I know he would hate an office job.'

'Will you be returning to Petersfield when he's well?'

To be honest, I haven't a clue. A short while ago Gerald and I had a letter from our house tenants asking us if we would consider selling the house as they were now in position to buy one and would like first refusal as it is so convenient for the veterinary practice. I talked about it with Gerald and was quite surprised that he didn't dismiss it out of hand. At least he is being realistic and accepts the fact that he will not return to the practice, and without that, there is little to keep him in Petersfield. We have no family there.

I have since arranged for a valuation on the house so we can at least have something to base our decision on.

'I'll be sad when you leave, you know.'

Mrs Dyer is being quite unguarded this morning with just the two of us here.

'It's been good having you here. I didn't really want a lodger to start with but now I'm not sure what I'll do when you go. I suppose I'll have to advertise for another working lodger and hope they're a good worker like you.'

'Or have some Land Girls,' I say, and she just pulls a face.

The conversation starts me pondering what the future holds for us. It will surely be only a few months more of hospital for Gerald, all being well. I realise we should be making plans. If we do sell the house in Petersfield we won't even have anywhere to live, but at the same time, finding where we want to live will depend on the kind of work Gerald can find. It looks like the war will be dragging on for a while which will impact on our prospects too.

Personally, I've become used to the Island and wouldn't mind settling here, with its mild climate and beautiful scenery. Not that I've been able to explore much, except this area, but Gerald doesn't know it at all and I imagine he won't be too keen on being so cut off from the mainland. Jobs might be difficult for him here too. We need to have some very frank discussions I think.

After we finish milking the cows, we wander back to the yard where Jack is hanging around the hay barn trying to persuade some hens to peck some corn from his hand.

'Come on Jack,' I say, 'let's go and see if there's any post today.'

He trots along beside me, stamping in muddy puddles, to the

farm postbox at the end of the drive. There are two letters in the box. One addressed to Jack, postmarked Clacton, which he takes and skips back to the farm ahead of me, while I look curiously at the other very official-looking letter addressed to Mrs Dyer. At the top of the envelope is printed, HMP Winchester.

In the kitchen I pass the letter to Mrs Dyer, who looks at it wide-eyed and gives me a worried look. She folds the envelope and tucks it into the breast pocket of her shirt before turning away and pouring us all porridge.

'Can you read Mum's letter with me?' Jack asks, oblivious of Mrs Dyers discomfort.

'Let's just have our porridge and then we'll read it together.'

I slit the envelope open for him and let him have a go at reading. His reading has made good improvement since he's been at the school, but he has difficulty with his Mum's handwriting, which, I must admit, is not the clearest. I help him.

Dear Jack.

Thank you for your letter and we're glad you enjoyed Christmas on the farm. You are keeping very busy with all the animals, especially with two lots of piglets to look after. Quite the little farmer now, aren't you! It was nice for you to get a new jumper and some games. I hope you said thank you properly.

Jack looks slightly affronted and says to me, 'I did say thank you properly, didn't I?'

'Yes, of course you did,' I reassure him. He is actually a very polite boy for his age.

It was so cold here at Christmas, frosty all day long, ice on the roads and some sleet and snow. Bert's cousin Emily and her husband John joined us for Christmas dinner and we also had a chicken that Bert managed to get through a works scheme. It was all a bit of a squash round the kitchen table, but we managed it.

Now, I have some exciting news for you. You're going to have a new baby brother or sister in March. What do you think about that?

I'm almost as astonished as Jack. He turns to me, checking that he's understood. 'Mum's going to have a baby?'

'Yes. That's a surprise, isn't it, Jack.' I wonder what he thinks about that news as I go on with the letter.

Bert and I were married in a registry office in October, so now Bert is your step-Dad. We'll be staying here while the war lasts, but we've got our names on the list for a council house back in London, so when that happens you'll be able to come back and join your new family.

In the meantime, we're trying to see if there's a way you could come and see us during the Easter holidays, but you'll have to sleep on the sofa. There's a man that works at Bert's place who delivers ship parts to Portsmouth docks on a regular basis. If someone can get you to Portsmouth, he can bring you back here. I can't promise anything, though, and we still have to work out how to get you back. That will be nice, won't it?

Write again soon, son.

Regards to the people at the farm.

Love Mum and Bert.

'Mum's having a baby! And what's a registry office?' Jack asks me. 'It's just a place where people can get married, instead of a church.' I tell him, but it's clear that it is just a minor thing that is on his mind.

'I don't really want to go back to London,' he says. 'I like it here. And I don't much like Bert,' he adds, 'He makes fun of me.'

'Well, Jack, it doesn't look as if the war will be coming to an end just yet, so you might be here for a little while. Things could change at Easter. You may be able to visit Clacton and you might think differently about things then when you see everyone and get to hold a new baby brother or sister.'

He pulls another face.

'Also, my husband should be better then and we will have to move to somewhere new as well'.

I put an arm around his shoulders.

'Don't scowl like that, your Mum will be really pleased to see you and you can tell them all about the farm and your new school here. You'll have so much to tell them. I bet you'll like the baby too.'

'Babies are smelly and cry all the time.'

'Not all the time, Jack. Sometimes they gurgle and smile too. Besides, you were a baby once!'

He pouts and kicks the chair leg.

I change the subject and tell him we have work to do outside and he can help me clean out the cow barn, so go and get his boots on.

I raise my eyebrows at Mrs Dyer and she gives me a similar look back.

Jack and I leave her to look at her own letter in private. I'm very curious but I will have to wait to see if she raises the subject.

CHAPTER 16

UNCERTAIN FUTURES

Elsie.

Elsie slits open the officious-looking letter, her heart beginning to race. Whatever it's about, she's sure it won't be good news.

She reads it through once quickly as a trickling of icy water creeps down her spine. She reads it more thoroughly and the ice pushes into her gut. It seems that Arthur is being transferred from Winchester to the Island Prison to serve his sentence. He'll be arriving on the 10th January. Just a couple of weeks!

She hadn't expected that. As he started off in Winchester, she expected him to stay there and he was safely out of sight and out of mind. Now, with the prospect of him being local, she fears he'll be asking her to visit occasionally.

Apart from immediately after he was sentenced, when there were financial issues to sort out, she hasn't heard from him and nor does she want to. And neither does she want to see him. She has moved on from their somewhat difficult marriage, even though life at the moment is no picnic and while he is across the water it is easy for her to push him out of her mind. If he'll be residing up the road from now on, she feels sure she'll feel his presence peering over her shoulder all the time, whispering criticisms and unwanted advice into her brain. He might even be more inclined to write to her or want something of her. She can imagine he might start poking his nose into her management of the farm.

Although it is still legally in his name, she regards it as her own. She stuffs the letter into the bureau drawer along with all the other official letters regarding Arthur's incarceration. Perhaps she is over-worrying. Maybe he won't be bothered about the farm or even about her. He was never particularly concerned about her well-being after all.

She remembers one time when she took a fall in the cow shed and put her back out. For some days it was painful to walk, bend, lift and twist, but she managed as best she could and there was never even one enquiry from Arthur about how her back was, or any extra help from him to do the heavy chores.

Sometimes she wonders at her own sanity for agreeing to marry him. In hindsight she knows she could have managed somehow quite well on her own, and might even have found a kinder partner if she had given herself more time, but back then, with her father bringing the tree nursery to a close, which had not been making a profit for some time, Elsie had felt the pressure to find herself new employment and somewhere to live. Her father bought himself a flat in a retirement complex, passing on a very modest inheritance to her to find herself some other security.

She had already met Arthur a few times and he came across as a fairly decent fellow, and managing a farm was an attractive option at the time. They did, in fact rub along quite well in the early years, but she gradually felt more and more taken for granted and any warmth between them soon evaporated.

She admits to herself that perhaps she wasn't the ideal wife either. Maybe Arthur would have preferred someone more feminine, a wife who would change into something more attractive of an evening, wear makeup, walk into town in a dress and heeled shoes. Not that he ever asked Elsie to do such things and she was quite comfortable in Arthur's old shirts and trousers, and too dog tired by the end of the working day to magic herself into something more desirable.

All that was immaterial, in her way of thinking, compared with the thing Arthur was prepared to do for his own self gain.

Elsie heads out to look for Helen. They need to do some more muck-spreading. Perhaps if Helen takes another dive into the heap it will lift her spirits.

Helen.

I wake on this January morning thinking I've overslept. In spite of the blackout curtains, the room seems lighter than usual. I peep outside and the world is white. So beautiful. My breath clouds the window as I view the changed scenery below and I hug my dressing gown across my chest.

I hurry down to the kitchen for a warm cup of tea, feeling thankful we are not milking the cows at 5 am at the moment. We have another hour or two in bed before we brave the elements.

I've never been so cold as this last month, outdoors mucking out the cow shed, the pigsty, clearing ditches, muck spreading, collecting pig swill. I've had to harden myself up. There's no room for whingeing when Mrs Dyer is about who doesn't seem to feel the cold. I don't think I'd survive in the north. We are about as far south as one can get in this country and I think it's cold! At least it's dry but the cold wind blasts off the channel, whipping over the downs and wheedling its crafty path through all my woolly layers to the very marrow of my bones.
I stand warming my buttocks on the range while I wait for the kettle to boil.
'Morning. And a beautiful one it is too. Have you looked outside?' Mrs Dyer rubs her hands and has a peek through the black-outs.
'Mmm, deep and crisp and even, isn't that what they say? I think we can turn the lamp off and open these curtains, let the day begin'.
She seems surprisingly cheerful this morning, whereas, although I agree it's a wondrous sight to see the first virgin snow, the thought of trudging out in the freezing cold is not filling me with enthusiasm.

A whooping whirlwind comes dashing down the stairs. 'Aunty Helen, Mrs Dyer! It's snowing!'

'Yes, we've noticed.'

'I'm going to make a snowman. Can I go out now, before breakfast?'

Jack makes me laugh with his innocent enthusiasm as we bundle him into Arthur's cut-down overcoat, Christmas hat, scarf and gloves and shoo him out the door. I watch through the window as he makes determined boot prints in the pristine snow and starts building his snowman.

'Well, Mrs Dyer. What's the plan for today?' At least muck-spreading will not be on the agenda, otherwise it will lie frozen on the top of the snow.

'I think we'll sort the animals out first, give them all some extra bedding to keep out the cold and check the troughs aren't iced over, then I think it's time we give the milking shed a good spring-clean so it's all ready when the calves start arriving. I know it's not yet, but there'll be other jobs to do when we thaw out.'

I'd like to ask Mrs Dyer if she's heard anything from Arthur since he came to the Island. She told me that he was being transferred. I suspect that she's finding it helpful to have someone like me to confide in, as she doesn't appear to be so 'closed in' on herself these days. Without any friends around here that she's willing to be close to, it must be very lonely keeping all her troubles and worries to herself, especially as she thinks others are all judging her for her husband's misdemeanors, whatever they were.

I haven't noticed any HMP letters arriving since that first one, and Mrs Dyer seems quite cheerful at the moment, so I guess she hasn't heard anything. I'm reluctant to ask. I don't want to pry.

By the time we break for lunch I'm surprised how warm I am, after moaning to myself earlier about how cold it was this morning. I feel quite ashamed.

We worked hard cleaning all the muck off the walls of the milking shed, scraping the floor and giving the walls a lick of whitewash.

After a corned beef hash for lunch, I clean myself up and head down to the chest hospital. With the snow still lying, not exactly deep but enough to soak my feet if I wear my shoes, I elect for my gumboots and take a pair of shoes in my bag.

Since mid December Gerald has been allowed walks around the hospital grounds which he's thrilled about and for a couple of weeks now he's been working a few afternoons in the greenhouses, potting up shrubs and planting seeds. All gentle work but he's so much more cheerful and I'm beginning to see a little healthy colour in his cheeks.

On my way I decide that the time has come for us to have a frank talk about the future.

Previously we decided between us that we would sell the Petersfield house and I've received several pieces of paperwork from the solicitor, although Christmas has slowed everything down. We've discussed the few items of furniture that we really want to keep - a dressing table and chest of drawers that came from my late mother, and Gerald's favourite wing-backed chair - but the rest of it we've offered to the Fields at a very fair price. We still have all our personal belongings boxed up and stored in the loft, so when we are ready to sign contracts I have to organise a removal van to empty it all. At this point I'm not sure where we will take it, but I believe there are some storage facilities on the Island. This is all work that Gerald and I would have organised together, but although we discuss it when I visit him, I am still doing the donkey-work, which suits neither of us.

By the time I reach the hospital, my gum boots are rubbing my heels and I begin to wonder if they were such a good idea.

Gerald is in the day room, reading a paper. 'Hello Darling.' I greet him.

He stands and gives me a kiss. 'Just scouring the situations vacant! Nothing much on offer that I can do.'

'I'll see what other papers or magazines I can bring. The farming magazines may have situations vacant.'

'I expect they'll just be full of labouring jobs as there's such a short supply now. There's just nothing else I can really do if I'm not a veterinary.'

I want to say that Gerald is being a little negative about things today, but I button my lip. It will be another two months before his final assessment so there's still time enough for him to find some employment, although no doubt the time will fly. I'd just like him to look more positively towards the future.

I leave the subject of employment for now and try another tack. 'What about somewhere to live when you finally get discharged? It may be better if we rent a simple flat somewhere round here and both find some local employment to pay the bills while we look around for something more permanent. Maybe when the war is over.'

'God knows when that'll be, Helen. I do listen to the news, you know.'

Oh dear, I think. Perhaps today is not a good one for these conversations, but it's a subject that is not going away, so I persevere.

After an hour and a half talking ourselves around in circles, the light is beginning to fade so I use it as an excuse to leave. I borrow a pair of Gerald's thickest socks to pad out my gum boots and head back to the farm.

I don't think Gerald has fully come to terms with the fact that he will struggle to cope with a veterinary job like he had before, and is reluctant to consider sedentary work. I can understand his reticence as he is an outdoor person, but when needs must, we have to do things we don't particularly like, at least for a while. He was also reluctant to embrace the idea of renting a flat temporarily, rather expecting that we would fall straight back into a house of our own. I think five months cooped up in hospital has divorced him from the realities of the world, especially the hardships of the war. It looks like I might have to come up with the ideas. I slog back to the farm in a pensive mood.

Mrs Dyer is in the yard when I arrive. 'Hello Helen. How was Mr Day this afternoon?'

'Getting better by the day, I think, and happier now he's more mobile and has work to do. He's working in the greenhouses which is fairly gentle work, but, all being well he should be able to do light work outside from next week. That will please him.'

'And what do you think he will do when he's finally able to leave?'

'Now that, Mrs Dyer, is a moot point! We talked ourselves round in circles this afternoon, and I'm afraid Gerald seems a little unrealistic about the immediate future.'

Mrs Dyer raises her eyebrows.

'For example, he's reluctant to think about our accommodation other than expecting us to suddenly move into another perfect house. And as he also seems to be anticipating a tailor-made job, he's in for quite a disappointment.' I sigh. I shouldn't really moan about Gerald like this. He's been through a lot, but I feel a new and fairly urgent weight on my shoulders and in spite of uneasy feelings of disloyalty, it's a relief to unburden myself to a neutral person in the shape of Mrs Dyer.

She commiserates with me.

'It looks like it's down to you, then, girl! Come on in, I found a bottle of sloe gin in the cupboard that I was saving for Christmas but forgot about, so let's have a tipple right now.'

We walk companionably back to the kitchen, past a row of ever decreasing snowmen. Jack has kept himself amused for a few hours and is now fast asleep on the sofa after his exertions in the snow.

One glass of sloe gin leads to another one as we sit companionably around the kitchen table discussing the troubles of the war, hopes and aspirations and the trickiness of negotiating around relationships.

With my slightly loosened tongue, it feels like an invitation to ask about Mr Dyer.

'Have you heard any more about your husband being transferred, Mrs Dyer?'

'Oh, let's drop the 'Mrs Dyer', now, shall we? We know each other better now. Call me Elsie. After all, I call you Helen.

Since you ask, I'm relieved to say I haven't heard a word from Arthur, but somehow I can't imagine it will be long before I do. I certainly don't want to see him. I have no time for scum like him.'

'And what did he do to deserve a prison sentence, Elsie?' I venture, but at that moment Jack wanders into the kitchen rubbing his eyes and asking,

'When's tea?'

Mrs Dyer lookes at the mantle clock.

'Goodness, Helen, I've been sitting here burdening you with the family secrets and we haven't got the tea ready yet. After three glasses of sloe gin, I hope I'm still capable!'

I laugh.

'I'm sure we can cobble something together between us!'

Jack

It was such fun today seeing the snow and it was deep enough to make snowmen. I made four altogether, although the last two were quite small as I'd used most of the good snow outside the kitchen. I didn't even feel cold. Mrs Dyer brought me some old carrots that she keeps for the horses, so I could use them for snowmen noses. I pinched some coal from the bunker for their eyes. I found the old dish in the barn that Mrs Dyer uses to catch blood from the dead rabbits and put it on my snowman for a hat. The others went without. I hope they all stay frozen until tomorrow because Jimmy is coming to play with me and he'll be impressed.

I had a letter from Mum. She wants me to go to Clacton at Easter but I don't really want to go. I think it will be nice to see Mum, but she'll have a baby and I suppose she'll spend all her time coo-cooing over it.

She said I might have to travel with a man in a lorry which could be good but I haven't met this man so I can't see how I'm supposed to go with him. How will I know who he is?

I wish Mum could come and see me instead. And now she's married Bert so I suppose he's my step-Dad. He'll make even more fun of me now. He'll mention me being a 'little' farmer in a mocking sort of way as if it's something I really believe I am, not something I'd like to be one day. Then he'll think of something about farms that he thinks is really witty and will laugh, even though he isn't funny. I kick the snow angrily into an arc of white slush.

Aunty Helen said she'll probably be moving to somewhere new at Easter with her husband. That makes me sad. It won't be the same at the farm without her. Just me and Mrs Dyer who is sometimes friendly but other times I feel invisible. I don't want Easter to come.

Elsie

January wears on and the war continues. Planes crossing the Channel, both our boys and the enemy, are commonplace sights. Regular gun booms from across the sea, echo off our high cliffs.

The town is full of troops, billeted here and there, with many coming in from St Lawrence and Niton where there are barracks and a canteen for the forces.

Fuel is becoming short, along with other essentials and more foodstuffs too.

The underground station outside the Bank of England has been blown up with considerable loss of life, Plymouth has suffered a massive night raid and every evening Elsie and Helen listen to heavily censored reports of the world-wide battles. They have to only imagine what they are not hearing.

On the farm and on this island they are largely protected from the hardships and grief of the war and for that Elsie counts her blessings and spares many thoughts for the millions facing homelessness, hunger, grief, injury and death, especially all the armed forces and front line nurses stalwartly doing their duty for their countries. She vows to put as much energy in as possible to produce all the food she can on her acreage and do her bit for the war effort.

When the Ministry men delivered all their recommendations and requirements, she felt slightly peeved knowing how tough it would be, but as the war wears on, she realises how much everyone has to make an effort if the country is going to get through this.

After the early cold snap of snow, ice and unusually plummeting temperatures, when even Elsie was feeling the bite in her fingers and toes, the weather turned mild and wet again.

She took the opportunity, with Simmy and Helen, to steer the newest pigs into the orchard to root up the rough ground so they could plant potatoes as suggested by the Ministry man.

She managed to order, from the local Agriculture committee, plenty of early seed spuds which she now has chitting in the barn and which, given some mild weather she'll get planted at the end of next month. By about that time, the first of the cows should start to calve, so she can see that March will be a particularly busy time. This brings her to worry about Easter time. She can't afford for Helen to leave at the moment unless she pays for more labour. She's already made considerable inroads into the overdraft, without paying extra wages.

She has to admit that not only has Helen proved to be a grafter on the farm, being willing to turn her hand at everything (except gutting rabbits!), but Elsie has felt happier with her company. Someone living in the house taking on some of the regular chores, someone to take responsibility with Jack, someone to talk to of an evening and who has a sense of humour. She realises now how lonely it was after Arthur left, with the whole responsibility of the farm on her shoulders.

Right now, she can't find any enthusiasm for advertising for a new lodger and the thought of having land girls still upsets her as she's aware her temperament might not suit the role of amiable boss, keeping young girls in check.

Earlier in the month she found Helen scanning the local paper for companies advertising storage as she needed to travel up to Petersfield to finalise their house sale and empty it of their belongings.

'How much stuff have you got?' she asked Helen.

'A van-load, I guess. Only three pieces of furniture, not too big, and the rest in boxes, our clothes, ornaments, kitchen things and so on.'

'Well, come and look in the dairy with me. Obviously we're not using the space now the cheese-making is finished. Will all your stuff fit in here? There's plenty of empty shelves.'

They assessed the space and decided that the furniture would be in the way, but all the boxes would fit fairly easily. They agreed that the furniture could be stored under a tarpaulin in the machine shed where Arthur used to keep his motorbike. She suggested a couple of mouse and rat traps to keep the vermin from nesting in Gerald's best armchair.

That decided, it was one less thing that Helen had to organise and pay for and she duly took a trip back to her old home to sign all the papers and supervise the loading of the van.

Elsie now wonders if she can persuade Helen to stay on for a while after her husband leaves hospital. Even if they lived in town, perhaps Helen would come and work each day. Perhaps they might both stay at the farm although Elsie is not sure that would feel comfortable, especially as Elsie has never met Gerald. From what Helen says, though, her husband doesn't sound too keen on staying on the island.

Elsie returns the tractor to the shed in the fading light, after taking bales of hay up to the horses. She pauses to admire Helen's handiwork of the afternoon where she's cleared the bottom quarter of the near field of encroaching thistles. It's a tough job that needs regular attention and one she tends to put off.

Helen is on tea-making duty today, enrolling Jack to make cheese and potato cakes with baked beans which gives Elsie time available to bed down all the livestock before night sets in. She walks round to check on the pigs. The youngsters are a lively bunch that's for sure. Even this late they are still bustling about shoving their snouts at the sow's underbellies trying to extract a last drink. They regularly break out of the field and she finds one or the other rooting around in the dung heap or other places they shouldn't be, giving her the run around as she tries to shepherd them, squealing, back where they belong. She mollifies herself with the thought that they will bring in a tidy income in a couple of months.

As she leaves, the air-raid siren wails out. She hasn't heard it in a little while so she stands to listen in the quiet of the descending night as the sound of planes travels on the wind across the water. It is shortly followed by other planes coming from the north. The RAF flying out to head off the enemy.

She hears the rat-tat of gunfire, the whine of plane engines spiralling out of control. She watches as a plane zooms out of the gloom heading towards her, engine sounding sick. The flare of flames follows it down and she sees it disappear to the west of the main road before a muffled explosion reaches her ears a split second before she witnesses the fire ball. She stands stock still for a moment. It was too dark to have seen whether the plane was enemy or British, but either way she feels a pit in her stomach at the fate of the airman.

She watches the darkness engulf her for several minutes as the sound of planes heads towards the east, overtaken by local sirens and emergency service bells. She walks back to the farmhouse with heavy steps, wondering how long this war will go on.

Indoors she finds Helen and Jack sitting under the stairs, Helen reading a fairytale. 'Thought it best to take cover,' Helen said.

At least Jack isn't freaked out by the air-raid siren anymore, like he was after his experience in the shelter and very soon the all-clear is sounded.

'Just watched a plane coming down over near the golf course,'

Elsie tells them. 'Exploded in a ball of fire, but it was too dark to see what it was. I didn't see a parachute or anything. Poor bugger.'

CHAPTER 17

THE GERMAN

Jack

It's another chilly morning and I dash outdoors to collect eggs and feed the hens and pigs before breakfast. My breath clouds out in front of me and my fingers are already freezing. If I wear my gloves I might drop the eggs so I've stuffed them in my pocket.

The hens aren't laying so well and Mrs Dyer says it's just because they are cold.

I head to the stable to fetch the corn and pig feed. The bolt isn't pushed across like it should be. The door is closed but I'm sure I bolted it properly. Mrs Dyer has drummed it into me to check it so that it doesn't blow open and allow the hens to sneak in. I wonder if she or Aunty Helen have been in and forgotten to bolt it properly.

I push the door open and check everything is as it should be, before scooping the feed out of the bin.

I hear a scuffling at the back in the shadow. A rustling of the straw. Something much bigger than a rat. I peer into the gloom but I can't see anything but I suddenly feel scared.

I'm about to hurry out and get Mrs Dyer when a figure emerges in a grey uniform. I'm not sure which of us looks most frightened and I try to scream but nothing comes out of my mouth.

The man's uniform is blackened and scruffy, his jacket unbuttoned and his shirt collar loose. His hair is really short but the worst thing about him is his face. Half of his head is red, bloody and oozing all down one side. One eye is partially closed, his cheek red raw with huge blisters and puffy, and his mouth is swollen. He's really scary.

It feels like it's forever that we are standing like this, me rigid with fright staring at his ghastly face, and him muttering something at me like "wasser, bitte, wasser". Finally he mimes having a drink and at that point I make a dash for the door.

'Mrs Dyer, Aunty Helen!' I shout as I dash across the yard, glancing back at the stable to see if the man is coming after me.

The scullery door opens and Mrs Dyer looks out. 'What's up, Jack?'

'There's a German in the stable and he wants water.'

I dash to the safety of the doorway.

'He's got a really scary face. It's all red and bloody and he's all in a mess.' I gabble my words out in a rush.

'Jeepers', Mrs Dyer says, as she turns and unhooks her gun from the wall and heads to the stable with a determined stride.

Aunty Helen comes hot on her heels, struggling to put her coat on. 'Stay here Jack.'

'He needs water,' I shout after her, and as she passes the yard pump, she quickly fills the tin mug kept beside it.

I watch from the safety of the doorway as Mrs Dyer cautiously opens the stable door wider with one hand and pokes the gun through with the other.

'Put your hands up', she bellows into the doorway.

Aunty Helen cautiously follows behind Mrs Dyer.

In a moment Aunty Helen comes running out, tin mug in hand. She turns me back to the kitchen.

'Run upstairs, Jack, and fetch the spare blanket out your wardrobe.'

By the time I return she has grabbed her purse and done her coat up.

'Take the blanket to the stable, and fetch another mug of water.' She thrusts the tin mug into my hand. 'I must dash down to the telephone box.'

I do as she says but I'm a bit nervous.

I call out, 'Mrs Dyer, can I come in? I've got a blanket and some water'.

She calls me to come in. She's resting against the feed bin with the gun propped at her side looking quite relaxed. The German is sitting against the partition between the two stables. He looks cold and ill.

'Good lad. Do you want to give them to the man? He won't hurt you.'

I'm not too sure about that but I place the things near his feet and step back quickly.

The German pulls the blanket tightly around himself, clearly trying to get warm. As I pass him the water he tries to smile but I can see it hurts his scabby face. He says, 'Danke, Danke,' which I presume means thank you.

I stand beside Mrs Dyer as he gulps the water noisily, much of it dripping out of his puffy mouth. He looks very young.

'Was he in that plane you saw last night?' I ask Mrs Dyer.

'I expect he was, son, but I don't think he can speak any English and I don't know German. It looks like it hurts him to speak. He needs to get to a hospital.'

'Is he dangerous?'

'Not at the moment. He's cold, hurt, and probably quite frightened. I know he's our enemy, Jack, but most of them are still human.'

'But he was trying to bomb us.'

'Sometimes people have no choice but to do as they are told by much nastier people.' She takes the mug that is offered by the German who says, 'Danke Frau'.

'What's your name? Namen?' She asks him.

'Reiner. Reiner Weber.'

'Well, Reiner, we'll be getting you to hospital. Hospital?'

The man nods his understanding. 'Yah, Danke, Frau.'

After what seems a long time we hear the clanging of an ambulance approaching and the whine of a police car and before long the yard feels full of people.

139

Mrs Dyer goes out to meet the police officers.

'He's young and hurt and needs medical attention. He's not armed.'

We stand to one side while they bring the man outside, still wrapped in the blanket, and deposit him in the ambulance with two officers at his side.

Aunty Helen ushers me back inside after that to have my breakfast and get ready for school so I'm not able to hear what the policemen have to say to Mrs Dyer.

I'll have a story to tell at school today. I think Jimmy might be impressed.

Helen

What a day it is. Quite an event for us this morning when Jack came running, shouting that there was a German in the stable. Mrs Dyer had her wits about her immediately as she grabbed the gun and headed out with purposeful strides to meet the enemy head on. I couldn't let her tackle the situation alone so I ran after her even though my heart was pounding.

It was clear that the German posed no threat, crouched as he was in the shadow with a burnt and bloodied face and in dreadful pain. You could see it in his eyes. He was most desperate for water more than anything, and I got Jack to fetch him another mugful before I hurried down to the telephone box for the emergency services.

I was glad, and perhaps unfairly surprised that Mrs Dyer showed him some compassion rather than prodding him with a gun or locking him in. After all, he was not much more than a boy, and the burns on his face were really quite severe. I doubt he will get away without scarring.

After Jack's initial shock he was very excited about seeing his first enemy German and couldn't wait to get to school to tell everyone of his adventure. I guessed the news would be all round the town before long.

I soon find out that I was right. When I take Biddy and the cart into town to collect the pig swill, Mary Bailiss, who works at St Catherine's School, comes out to help me.

'Hello Mrs Day, hear you had some excitement up at the farm this morning', she greets me.

'Yes we did. News travels fast I see!'

She folds her arms, settling in to wait for the gossip.

I tell her the bare bones of the story, although she knows the facts already, just wants to hear it from the horse's mouth.

'Bet that Mrs Dyer gave him a mouthful.'

'No, Mrs Dyer was very cool and collected. The German was quite young and in a lot of pain.'

'Well, only what he deserves.'

I take my leave fairly promptly after that remark. People understandably have little compassion for Germans no matter who they are or their circumstances.

It's late afternoon before we clop back into the yard where I see an Austin 10 parked and two men talking to Mrs Dyer.

I jump down from the cart as Mrs Dyer introduces me to the men.

'This is Mrs Day who works with me.'

Turning to me she rolls her eyes.

'These men are from the Island News. They want a story about the German. I've given them the gist of it, although I think they were expecting more drama.'

'Mrs Dyer,' one of the men speaks up. He's brandishing a large camera with flashbulb attached.

'We need a photograph to go with the story. Could you stand over by the stable, with the gun in your hand, perhaps.'

'Certainly not!' Mrs Dyer is quite indignant. 'I don't want my face in any newspaper.'

The photographer is quite put out.

'We really need a photograph, Mrs Dyer. I'll make sure you're quite happy with it before we use it.'

I have an idea that may mollify both of them.

'Why don't I get Jack? After all, he's the one that first discovered

the airman and I'm sure he'd love his photograph in the paper.'
I look pointedly at the cameraman.
'Pictures of children sell papers, don't they?'
It's agreed all round and I go inside to call Jack down from his bedroom. Of course, he's thrilled to have all the attention and gladly poses in front of the stable for several different shots. He certainly has a disarming smile when he wants.
The two newsmen drive off, reasonably satisfied, although it's no surprise that Elsie is less than happy. 'Might have known we'd have the Press sniffing round. Pushy pair. Wanted to put all sorts of dramatic slants on the story and make the poor fellow out to be some devil in disguise. Bet they still write it up with plenty of embellishments that didn't happen. I could do without another round of town gossip.'
'Well I'm afraid to tell you, Elsie, they are already gossiping!'
I unhitch Biddy from the cart and Jack helps me unharness her, and fetch feed and straw for all the livestock. He chatters the whole time about the morning adventure.

CHAPTER 18

ARTHUR

Elsie

The following day Elsie walks down the end of the drive to the letter box with Helen and Jack as Helen goes off to work at Hugh Taylor's and Jack to school. Elsie stops to collect the post, just one letter today which she stares at with a sinking feeling in her heart. HMP Parkhurst, Isle of Wight. She knew she'd get one before long. She slits the envelope aggressively before she's even home.

Dear Else (There was no other person on this earth that called her Else)

As you know I've been transferred. I thought you might have come to see me by now, but it looks like I'll have to ask you.
It's a bit better here than Winchester, but that's not saying much. I have a cell to myself which is something but there's some nasty geezers in here.
You can bring me something nice to eat, cake or bread pudding like you used to make.
I want to know what you've been doing to the farm since I've been gone.
I've opened a government bank account in the prison as I need cash for essentials like ciggies, soap, razors and the like. You need to pay in some funds from the farm bank for me. I need to know what our financial situation is now, so can you apply for a visit soon as?

Your husband, Arthur. (In case you've forgotten who I am)

Elsie shoves the letter roughly back in the envelope.

All about him, she thinks. No enquiry how she is, and how she's coping after his abrupt departure. Just expectation that she'll drop everything to go running to the prison with cake, bread pudding and a wad of cash! Well, he can jolly well wait, she thinks. Let him stew on it for a while before she does any such thing. And if that toe-rag thinks he's getting more than a pittance, he can think again. She's managing on thin air at the moment, so can he.

She stomps back to the scullery in a mood and drags on her gum boots ready to join Simmy for the morning's work. They are clearing ditches and trimming the hedges at the top of the farm and some good hard graft is just what she needs now and to hack at a few overgrown hawthorns to vent her anger.

The following week, on the morning that Helen works on the farm books and other paperwork, Elsie decides to ask her to contact the prison governor requesting a visit.

'You heard, then.' Helen says matter-of-factly.

'I expect you'll probably have to fill in a form or two with all your details. I'll get on to it this morning.'

'He wants me to transfer money to him amongst other things.'

'What does he need money for, in prison?'

'Cigarettes, he says, and other essentials like soap and razors. Probably gambling or illicit booze as well. I can't imagine prison is turning him into a model citizen.'

'Elsie,' Helen ventures, 'What exactly did Mr Dyer do?'

At first Elsie just stares out the window and Helen wishes she hadn't asked.

'I'm sorry Elsie, perhaps I shouldn't have asked you.'

'No, it's fine. It's just that I've never divulged it to anyone else. I don't have friends to confide in. Never felt I needed them. I'll tell you over lunch, though.'

With that she leaves Helen to her paperwork and goes on out to the farm.

She spends the morning with Simmy, sawing the larger branches for logs for the lounge fire while Simmy enjoys warming his hands by the bonfire of twigs and smaller cuttings.

Most of the time Elsie's mind wanders over the events of last March. When she relates them to Helen over lunch, she intends to keep to the facts and try and keep her emotions out of it, although when it comes to talking about Arthur, she might find that difficult.

She remembers the night the whole world changed for her and Arthur. Until that time all she had were her suspicions. And as it turned out her suspicions were totally unfounded. Arthur was up to something much more sinister than a secret affair.

Arthur had left in the early evening on his fancy motorbike to do his usual trip to the RAF station with the cheese and milk and to collect the pig swill. He told her he would drop the cart back at the farm afterwards and then go for a pint with Billy Price. She knew from experience that usually meant a late night.

She busied herself all evening feeding and bedding the livestock, waxing the cheeses, cleaning the dairy. In the end she decided to retire to bed even though Arthur always wanted her to still be awake and downstairs on his return. As it happened, Arthur came home earlier than she expected and as she was just cleaning her teeth in the scullery sink, so she didn't have to confess to the fact she was about to go to bed.

It was barely fifteen minutes after they had turned the bedroom lamp off that Elsie heard engines and tyres on the gravel of the yard.

'Who on earth is that at this time of night?' she asked, mainly to herself as Arthur had already dropped off to sleep.

She dragged on her old dressing gown and peeked out of the blackouts. There were no lights but she could see by the weak moonlight that there were two cars below and several men were climbing out. Two walked around to the front while others stood in the yard looking up at the windows.

'It's police, Arthur,' she said, and he was instantly awake, leaping out of bed and dashing for the stairs, fastening his dressing gown as he went.

Elsie's heart was already hammering. A police visit was hardly going to be a social call. What had Arthur been up to?

There came an insistent knock at the front door by the time she reached the top of the stairs and Arthur was already unbolting it and pushing back the curtain.

Two officers walked in as Elsie lit the lamp. They flashed their identity cards at Arthur.

'Mr Arthur Dyer?'

'Yes, that's me', Arthur replied innocently.

'And Mrs Dyer?' One of the men looked in Elsie's direction. She nodded. She seemed to have lost her voice temporarily.

'How can I help you, officers?' Arthur asked.

Oh the gall of him, Elsie thinks now, as if he had no clue as to the officer's visit.

'Mr Dyer, I am arresting you on suspicion of aiding and abetting an enemy of the state.'

'What?'

Elsie's exclamation was out before the officer had even finished his speech. What was he talking about, aiding and abetting an enemy?

The officer ignored her.

'We need you to accompany us to the station to help with our enquiries.'

'I think you'll find this is all a mistake,' Arthur said.

'Can I go upstairs and put some clothes on?'

The senior officer nodded to his companion to follow Arthur.

Elsie found that her hands were uncharacteristically trembling.

'What's my husband supposed to have done?' she asked, sinking onto one of the hard backed chairs.

The officer looked at her, unsmiling and tight lipped.

'As I said, Mrs Dyer, we'll be questioning him at the station. In the meantime, you are to remain here as we may wish to question you too.'

Well, she was hardly about to leave the premises with twenty five cows in the middle of calving season.

She took a deep breath to steady her nerves and watched mutely as Arthur walked out in his overcoat and trilby between the two officers. He looked at her just once and gave a shake of his head as if it was all a mighty nuisance that would soon be resolved.

Elsie turned off the lamp and watched out the window as the cars were driven round to the front and Arthur was placed between two policemen in the back of the leading vehicle.

She sat again at the kitchen table in the dark, contemplating what it was all about.

Somehow she had a feeling that it was connected with Billy Price in some way. He was a shifty one, no doubt about that. If they had been thieving or getting themselves embroiled with black market dealings, she wouldn't have been totally surprised, but aiding and abetting an enemy? Maybe Arthur was right and it was all a mistake.

She finally took herself to bed but sleep was so long coming, it was only a couple of hours before she rose again to face the day.

Helen

This morning I could see how agitated Elsie was about visiting her husband. She would rather not think or speak about him at all. I wondered if she would actually tell me about his misdemeanours over lunch or whether she would clam up about him. It wasn't my place to pry so I wouldn't mention the subject again unless Elsie did.

She comes into the kitchen at lunchtime rubbing her hands and stamping her feet.

'Crikey, it's bloomin' freezing up the back end of the farm. Catching that cold wind.'

She sits at the table as I pour out the thick bean stew and she warms her hands around the bowl.

'Mmm, just the thing for a day like this. Nice to be waited on too! How have you got on this morning?'

I update her on the paperwork, orders placed, bills paid, filing done.

'I also took the liberty of walking down to the telephone box and calling the prison reception to ask about the visiting protocol. They are sending you a visitor application form and on receipt they will notify you of a date and time.'

'Thanks for that. Let's hope it's later rather than sooner!'

'When might he expect to be free?' I ask her.

'Free? He's lucky he hasn't had the noose around his neck! He's in for a very long time, Helen, charged under the Treachery Act for selling state secrets to the Germans.'

I look at her in amazement.

'He's a spy?'

'Nothing so intelligent. Just greedy and stupid when he saw a very lucrative opportunity. Makes no difference to the charge, though.'

'Did you have any idea, Elsie?'

'No. He'd been acting a little out of character for a while, staying out later at the pub and so on. I thought he was having an affair! I'm so naive!

The first I knew it was something more serious was when the police came and took him away for questioning. Even then I didn't know what he'd been up to until the following afternoon.'

She proceeds to tell me about being woken by the police coming to take her husband for questioning and how she had to rouse herself to work on the farm not knowing what it was all about.

She clears our lunch bowls and makes us a pot of tea which we share at the kitchen table.

'I was still up at the milking shed when those two policemen came back looking for me. They flashed a warrant card at me and told me they'd come to search the house. What for, I asked them, but they buttoned their lip, ushered me into the kitchen and proceeded to go through the place with a fine tooth comb. At the bureau they scrutinised every paper, turned the drawers upside down and felt all round for secret compartments I suppose. Then they went upstairs rummaging through our bedroom drawers. It was awful. They didn't say a word to me until they left, when they told me I would be hearing from them in due course. I still didn't know what they were looking for.'

We sip our tea.

'Gosh, it must have been really upsetting for you, especially not knowing what it was all about,' I say, not thinking of anything more useful to say at that point.

'Jeepers, Helen, having those two rummaging in my underclothes and moving all my personal things. It was ghastly.'

I begin to realise the weight that's been hanging around Elsie's shoulders.

'It was probably early afternoon when they came back. This time it was me they wanted down the station for questioning. Honestly, Helen, I felt like a criminal even though I hadn't done anything. Two of our labourers watched me being taken off in a police car. God knows what they must have thought. Well, I suppose I do know really, because they resigned soon after that.

I was taken into an interrogation room and sat facing two detectives across a small wooden table. First they asked me if I knew Arthur was selling secrets to a German agent, then they asked what I knew about the RAF station near us.

'Well', I said, 'we regularly sell our cheese and milk there and collect the swill for the pigs'. They wanted to know how often Arthur made the trip, who he knew there and what he'd told me about it. I didn't know anything really. 'What do you think the RAF station is there for?' they asked.

I only know what everyone in town must know, that the masts are for some kind of radio signals to listen in to the Germans and provide us with some sort of early warning. It's all kept very secret, but that seems to be the bones of it. I still don't know if there's anything more to it than that. It's what I told the officers because that's all I know.

They kept asking if Arthur had any particular contacts there and all I could tell them was that he sometimes shared a cigarette with the chap in charge of the canteen and who helped him load the swill bins.

Finally they asked me if I knew Billy Price. I knew he'd have something to do with it. I told them I did know Price and that I didn't much like him although Arthur was happy to have him as a drinking pal. That caused some interest. What didn't I like about him, they wanted to know. I said I just thought he was slightly shifty. What did I mean by shifty? What caused me to think that? On and on they went until they finally sat back and surveyed me with grim expressions. I don't mind telling you, Helen, I felt as guilty as hell by then, even though I still hadn't grasped the full facts.

Eventually they told me that Arthur had been making plans of the RAF base with details about the underground operations rooms and the personnel working there. All of it was top secret information and he had been selling it via an accomplice to a German agent. They wanted to know who was the accomplice and who was the agent. I think they knew that Billy Price was the accomplice but wanted me to confirm it. I was fairly sure myself but couldn't tell them for certain. As for a German agent, I hadn't the foggiest idea.

In the end I was allowed to leave, although no such thing as a lift back to the farm and by the time I'd caught a bus the poor farm men had had to do the milking and all the chores on their own.

'Goodness, Elsie, what a story.'

Poor woman, I think, being put through all that, and what a stupid naive husband.

'I still didn't know what was going to happen to Arthur at that stage and it was another day before a lone policeman came round to see me.

'Mrs Dyer,' he said, 'I've just come to inform you that your husband has been charged under the Treachery Act, for aiding and abetting an enemy of the state. He will be held in custody at

Newport until his trial at Winchester Assizes. You will be allowed to visit him between 2 and 4 on weekdays while he is in custody. He has already asked that you do so.'

The last thing I wanted to do was visit this traitor of a husband, but there were things we needed to discuss about the farm and the finances so, reluctantly, I did visit him. Twice in fact.

So that's my sorry story, Helen. Within a very short time the news spread to the town gossip mongers and my name was mud, even though I knew nothing about his dirty dealings.

Two of our men decided to enlist and left the farm, and the other two were perhaps more honest and told me outright they weren't prepared to have a woman as boss or to be associated with Warren Farm. Luckily Simmy was still loyal, and he managed to persuade old George to join us.'

She gives an enormous sigh and looks at the clock on the mantelpiece.

'Now this wretched man seems to be worming his way back into my life.'

She changes the subject.

'Time we set to work, Helen. By the way, how was your husband when you visited yesterday?'

Gerald is making really good progress. He's actually enjoying life at the moment as now he's feeling better in himself, it's like he's staying in a holiday hotel with all meals provided, good fresh produce from their own land, outdoor work that isn't too taxing, plenty of rests and companionship with other men. He's so far removed from the daily realities of the war. I have to gently remind him about rationing, fuel shortage, people working all hours to make ends meet. And here on the Island, we are the lucky ones. If we lived in London we'd have a much harder life, and if Gerald had been well, he might even be doing serious or dangerous war work.

Yesterday he met me in the communal lounge of the hospital full of the outdoor work he'd been doing, helping to rake out the pigsty and wheeling barrows of fresh straw. While the weather has been dry he's been outdoors most mornings, and then after a long rest he works for an hour in the greenhouses. He looks healthy, with colour in his cheeks and his weight has improved. He has much more to talk about during my visits and laughs more readily, especially if I relate some of the things we have to do on the farm.

I admit to feeling a little resentful when I slog back up the hills to the farm, considering the hours we put in every day and the heavy work we do. I have to remind myself that I do actually enjoy being here, even if the work is tough, and sometimes in the early mornings when it's as cold as it has been recently I wish I had a warm office job.

Gerald is due for another visit to the consultant when I hope he will have some idea of when he will be discharged. As it appears his lungs are much stronger now, I imagine he will be able to make some home visits soon. The trouble is, we haven't got a home at the moment.

I decided yesterday to broach the subject again.

'Gerald, you'll probably be allowed some home visits soon. Do you want me to look around for a short term rent somewhere. I don't know how Mrs Dyer would feel about it, but I could ask her if she minds you staying there sometimes. You would have to pay her rent, but it would be the easier option, wouldn't it? We could find somewhere permanent when you get a job.'

He pondered my suggestion for a while.

'It will just be for weekends to start with and then we have another assessment before we can return home for good. I suppose, if Mrs Dyer is agreeable, I could stay for weekends until I'm discharged. See what she says, Helen.'

It was a step in the right direction. He still isn't addressing the issue of what comes next.

I decided I would start scanning the papers and the country and farming magazines to see if I could pick out some jobs that Gerald may be fit enough to do. With that end, I diverted into the town to the newsagents and picked out the Farming Today paper and The Country magazine, treating Jack to a comic while

I was there.

I thought the town was beginning to look as weary as the population. Many of the shops were now boarded up. People looked tired and drab, women in old overcoats with scarves pulled tightly over their heads struggling with two bags of shopping, a few men on bicycles straining to balance heavy boxes strapped to the back and still some women queueing patiently at the greengrocers, even at that late hour. People hurried home with fixed expressions, no one stopping to chat companionably with neighbours or friends. That's except a few groups of army personnel who stood on corners smoking and enjoying their time off.

Light was fading by the time I left town and I hurried my step.

Jack.

When I told my classmates last week about the adventure with the German, I think they were a tiny bit jealous. They wanted to know all the details of what the man was like and I told the story lots of times. I enjoyed feeling important for a while. The local paper came out a few days later and I was actually on the front page! I took the front cover and showed it around to my mates. There was a big photo of me standing by the door to the stable and then a whole column about it which Aunty Helen read to me. I asked her if I could send it to my Mum and the next day she bought another paper so she could keep one for herself. With Aunty Helen's help, I wrote Mum a letter and enclosed the article. After I posted it I wondered if Mum would think it was too dangerous now for me to stay here and tell me I had to go to Jaywick after all. I hope not. She said she was going to arrange for me to visit during the Easter holidays, but I'd rather stay here.

Yesterday evening Aunty Helen brought me a comic to read which was nice. After tea I curled up on the sofa to read it while she and Mrs Dyer chatted in the kitchen over their pot of tea. I heard Aunty Helen ask her about Mr Day staying here. At least I think that's what it was about. She said he has to go home at weekends for a while until he is properly better. I don't know what Mrs Dyer said about it. It will feel a bit strange if Aunty Helen's husband comes here to stay. I wonder what he is like. I hope he's nothing like Bert.

I became engrossed in my comic after that and soon they both came into the lounge to listen to the wireless news.

Elsie.

Elsie hears from the prison this morning. Her visit date is 15th February, just five days from now. She's not at all happy about it. Apart from seeing her husband again, it's the inconvenience when she's got more than enough work to cope with. Just as well they are not milking or calving yet as it will take up half of her day travelling to Newport and back with two buses to catch each way.

She heads out to the cowshed thinking about the future. She wonders what Arthur will say about the farm. Perhaps he thinks he can give her orders about how to manage it. She scoffs inwardly at that thought. Just let him try! Maybe he wants her to sell up, and that sets her wondering where she stands on that. The farm is still in his name, so would he be entitled to all the profits? Surely her input over the years will count for something. She makes a mental note to try and find out her rights.

With all this on her mind and now Helen has asked if her husband can come here for weekends. Well, what could she say. It's obvious it makes the most sense and he wouldn't be taking up any more rooms. She already has their worldly possessions stacked in the redundant dairy and the barn. If he paid a rent for food and lodging, it would help her out at the moment as the finances are really tight until she receives some income again from the milk.

However, not having met the man, she feels uneasy about it. They had established a comfortable routine between Helen,

Jack and herself. She is not sure she wants to become used to something different.

While she shovels out the cow muck from the shed, she tries to think more positively. One of her downfalls is her lack of need for other people. She is quite aware that it makes her seem aloof or anti-social. Some would say quite rude, although she never really means to be. She prefers to work alone and dislikes delegating to other workers, although since Arthur's exit she has had to deal with that daily. The prospect of another change to her routine and another person to make welcome feels uncomfortable.

However, looking at her immediate prospects, things are not looking too good. She is just about managing to keep out of debt, apart from the bank overdraft, relying heavily on their home-grown produce, making do and mending - model wartime citizens, in fact, but if any unforeseen bills come her way, she will really struggle. She certainly can't be paying Arthur a regular amount from the farm profits, because there aren't any. She's hopeful that things will start to look up in the spring with milk for sale, potatoes to harvest, bull calves to send to market along with the piglets who should fetch a very decent price.

In the meantime, a weekend lodger like Mr Day will help a little, and if he's well enough now to carry out some light manual work at the hospital, perhaps he could lend a hand around the farm. With that thought she decides the sensible choice is to say yes to Helen.

The fifteenth of February comes around far too quickly. In the morning Elsie carries on as normal but the whole time her stomach feels full of birds and her mouth is dry. In the end, she just wants to get the prison visit over with.

After lunch she changes out of her dirty work clothes and finds a brown wool skirt and thick red cardigan that she can't remember the last time she wore. She shakes them out and checks the moths haven't been at them during their time in the wardrobe.

With a red felt hat pulled over her hair and her heavy old out-door coat on she feels both unaccustomly smart but uncomfortably constrained at the same time. She heads out to the bus stop.

Outside the prison door to which she has been directed, she waits with four other women for 2 o'clock.

She is aware of a few sideways glances, but no-one chats. Eventually a young woman says, 'Haven't seen you before.'

'No'. Elsie keeps her eyes ahead, she doesn't want to be drawn into conversation. A quick glance reveals the woman making a face at her neighbour and they leave her alone.

At two o'clock on the dot, they are allowed into the prison, to the first room where Elsie relinquishes her handbag to an officer who sorts through it methodically, carefully unwrapping the wedge of bread pudding and sniffing at it. After that, with arms spread wide she is patted down embarassingly to ensure she's not carrying a dangerous weapon stuffed down her knickers, and finally led through three more locked doors to the visiting room.

She stands a moment at the door before she sees Arthur at one of the individual tables near the far corner.

She sits down on the functional hard back chair opposite him.

It's ten months since she last saw him but he looks much the same, if a little thinner.

'Hello Else. Long time no see.'

'Hello Arthur. How are you?'

'Surviving.'

I brought you this.' She hands over the pudding.

'Great. Should be better than the slop we get in here. And cash? Have you brought cash with you?'

She draws her purse from the bag and pulls out some notes. It attracts the attention of the attending prison officer who walks over to see what is being passed across.

'It's just for ciggies and the like, officer,' Arthur tells him.

The man allows her to pass over a small amount of the cash.

'Money should be paid into the bank account from now on.'

Arthur tells Elsie that she can arrange a monthly payment to his account.

'It won't be much, Arthur. Things are really tight at the moment.'

'Why, what you been doing with the farm, then?'

Elsie takes a calming breath.

'In case you've forgotten, there's a war on, and when you left under a cloud the gossip mongers had a field day so most of our customers left too, as did the labourers. Babcock decided he was better off enlisting, Curran objected to a woman boss so went off to enlist too, and the two youngsters refused to be associated with Warren Farm anymore.'

'Disloyal rats!'

He's a right one to talk, she thinks.

'So you see, I was left with Simmy trying to manage everything. I closed the dairy down and sold half the herd.'

'You can't make a profit with half the herd, woman!'

'Exactly. The Ministry has been on my back so I've organised an overdraft to tide me over while I sort out all the extra things they expect. Half the acreage to be cultivated, mainly potatoes, silage crops and brassicas, and double the pig-rearing. We are just about on top of the work but it'll be spring before we start to have any return on the outlay. Things should ease a little when the milking comes back in and when the piglets are ready for market.'

'Have you taken on more labour?'

'I had to pay for temporary workers for the potato harvest and Simmy persuaded old George from the village to help at the evening milking'.

She takes a breath. She's not sure what Arthur will think of the next piece of news.

'I've also taken in a lodger who works for me full time, and I have a child evacuee too. I get an allowance for him.'

'A lodger? Who's that then?'

'Her name is Mrs Day. She works hard, in case you were wondering, and it's nice to have a bit of company too.'

'Christ! That sounds all very cosy, I must say. Got yourself quite a little family there, by the sound of it.'

'Yes, I have,' she says very pointedly, staring directly at him, her chin set firm. She suddenly feels much stronger in his presence than she ever did when they were together. Behind the little wooden table he seems somehow diminished now.

'When I get out of here, Else, they'll have to go. We'll soon increase the herd again and have the farm back as it was. We'll buy one of them new milking machines. Get the work done in half the time and then you can do the cheese again.'

The man is deluded, she thinks.

'Arthur, anything can happen in the next fifteen years.'

'I'll have parole by then, you'll see. Once this war's over.'

She hadn't gone to his trial at Winchester in April. Mainly she didn't want to, but fortunately she had a very valid excuse as she was still struggling with the whole herd to milk twice a day, and a trip to Winchester would take up a whole day, if not more, plus transport costs that she could ill afford.

She half expected the death sentence to be pronounced, but obviously his actions were small fry in the scheme of things and he was given fifteen years. When she thought of him being fifty-nine when he would complete his sentence she almost felt sorry for him. Gullible, stupid fool that he was. There was some satisfaction that Billy Price also went down for the same amount, but she had not heard that the enquiries had ever led to the discovery of the secret agent. So many things were hushed up these days, she would never be sure.

Today, to make small talk, she makes the effort to show some interest in his days at the prison and how it compares to Winchester, but soon finds herself watching the clock on the wall. It seems to tick round very slowly.

Finally she is able to leave.

'Well, take care of yourself, Arthur,' she manages to say as she buttons up her coat.

'Don't forget to pay in the money, Else,' his parting words follow her as she walks out the building with a huge sigh of relief. She reflects that there has not been a single enquiry about her well-being, no interest in her lodger or her evacuee, no thanks for taking the time to visit, no apology for putting her through all this. Just as he's always been, she thinks. It's all about him.

CHAPTER 19

HOME VISITS

Helen

At last Gerald will be coming home for the weekend, for two nights, starting today, Friday. When I think of 'home' it feels quite natural for me to mean the farm, but of course Gerald's home has been the hospital for seven months and the farm will be completely new for him. I feel quite anxious about his visit. What will he make of Elsie, and perhaps more to the point, how will she be with him. She isn't the easiest of people to feel comfortable with at first. There is also Jack. He freely calls me Aunty and I feel like I'm his real aunt, part of the same family. I will miss him terribly when we move away somewhere, or when it's time for him to return to his mother.

Gerald was supposed to be having his first weekend with us last week, but we had another spell of freezing weather, thick white frost in the mornings and even a day of snow which delighted Jack no end, even though it was a little thin to make snowmen. The hospital thought it best to postpone Gerald's visit. As for us, we were supposed to be planting early potatoes this week but it will have to wait until the ground has thawed. There's been plenty of other work to keep us warm and fit. The piglets are growing by the day and becoming like rebellious children. They constantly find a way through the fence and we end up chasing them across the farm trying to bring them back, at which time they squeal like mad as if we're murdering them. Patience wears thin after a while!

Elsie went to visit her husband at the start of the month and came back moaning about him that he hadn't changed one bit, and didn't appear the least bit remorseful about his actions. She said he was in denial about his sentence and seemed to think he would have it repealed as soon as the war is over. Elsie thinks that is very much wishful thinking. I'm inclined to agree as I've heard that aiding the Germans in any way is one of the most serious crimes anyone can do.

I'm to collect Gerald from the hospital at 2pm and Elsie has suggested I take the dog cart as it's too far uphill for Gerald to manage. I'm glad for that as I would have had to pay for a taxi otherwise. In return I offer to collect some goods from the hardware store, which I decide to do after I collect Gerald and that way I can meet Jack from school too. He usually walks back from school on his own now but it will give him and Gerald a chance to become acquainted without it being too intense.

As it's a special occasion, I change out of my dirty dungarees, don a thick skirt and a rather worn but still serviceable cable-knit jumper, and apply a little make-up for a change. I still need to wrap up warm, though. The frost may have gone but there's a chilly wind blowing off the sea.

I harness Biddy to the cart. I always choose Biddy to take me anywhere as, being older than the other horse, Pat, she tends to be less frisky and I trust her more. I feel more confident with a placid horse!

There are very few vehicles on the road as we make our steady way towards the hospital. The fuel shortage is having quite an effect and people are saving their coupons for emergencies. We limit the times we use the tractor on the farm, using the horses whenever practical.

I find Gerald reading the paper in his room and he greets me enthusiastically.

'Hello, my darling,' he says.

'We've been waiting a long time for this, haven't we?' He kisses me passionately and I wonder if this is a foretaste of things to come!

His bag is on the bed, open, but already packed with a change of clothes. His overcoat and scarf beside the bag, already to leave. It looks as if he is impatient to go, which is quite understandable.

'Ready for a change of scenery at last?' I ask.

'Yes, let's go. Have you ordered a taxi?'

'No. I'm afraid nothing so luxurious. You'll be coming down in the world on the cart.'

I tell him we're heading into town for errands and to collect Jack and he's pleased to have a guided tour of the town where he's been living for the last seven months.

'It's good to see the place you've been talking about all this time,' he remarks, taking in the aging Victorian architecture, the rows of houses balanced up the cliffside on zig zag roads and the constant views out to sea.

We drive past the Coop, still under repair, which brings back a few shivers down my spine.

'This was bombed in the air raid,' I tell him, but I continue to keep quiet about being caught up in it.

I collect my goods from the hardware store, luckily with no queue, and we make our way back towards the school.

Along with a sudden rush of noisy and jostling children dashing out of the school gates I see Jack, satchel slung crosswise over his chest, sandwiched between Jimmy and some other friends. I point him out to Gerald.

'Jack!', I shout, and he turns and sees Biddy and the cart.

'I didn't know you were coming, Aunty Helen,' he says as he climbs aboard and sits at the back.

I tell him that I've just collected Gerald and I introduce them both.

'Hello,' he says, shyly.

Gerald turns and shakes his hand.

'I'm very pleased to meet you, Jack. I've heard lots of good things about you and how good you are with all the farm jobs. There's a lot to do on a farm, isn't there?'

I'm very relieved at Gerald's easy way with Jack, and they continue to chat about the farm all the way home. I just hope things are as easy with Elsie.

We trot into the yard and I suggest Jack takes Gerald into the house to show him up to our bedroom, while I see to the horse. I guess Elsie will be out on the farm somewhere at this hour. I find her mucking out the stable when I lead Biddy back to the field and we feed and water the horses together.

'Your husband alright?' She asks.

I tell her he's excited about a change of scenery at last and we walk back to the house so she can meet him.

In the kitchen we find Gerald playing a game of rock, paper, scissors with Jack. He seems to have scored a hit with the lad already.

'Ah, Mrs Dyer. Lovely to meet you and I'm very grateful to you for letting me stay here.' My husband certainly knows how to make a smooth impression.

Elsie nods at him. 'Pleased to meet you, I'm sure,' she says rather formally, and moves to the cooker, banging some pans around.

'Hope you like rabbit, Mr Dyer. It's pretty well compulsory in this house.'

I'm reluctant to leave our cosy bed in the morning at the usual hour, after our first night together for so long.

We lay together last night for a long time whispering into the night, catching up with each other on a more intimate level. Our first efforts to make love, ended with Gerald feeling frustrated at his inability to perform as he wished. I told him that it was early days and encouraged him to cuddle me tightly and just enjoy the feeling of our skin on skin, and we gently fell asleep like that.

Later in the night we woke and the warmth of the bed, our sleep-relaxed bodies, a passionate kiss and our love-making resumed, both of us giggling as we tried to keep the bed from squeaking, knowing Elsie was sleeping in the next room. I felt as if I had my husband back again at last.

It's gone six when I try to creep out of bed without waking Gerald, but he is awake in an instant.

'You stay there, love,' I say. 'Enjoy a lie-in and I'll see you at breakfast time. I ought to give Elsie a hand.'

'I can see what you mean about Mrs Dyer. She's quite abrupt at times isn't she? And it's difficult to feel at ease with her. I thought I did my best yesterday, though! Perhaps she's just shy.'

'Yes, it took me a while, but now we've lived together all this time, she's much easier company. She even has a sense of humour sometimes, I promise you!'

I dress hurriedly.

'Good grief, Helen,' Gerald says from the bed, 'what are you wearing!'

I give him a twirl, wearing my grubby dungarees and baggy sweater.

'I'll hardly be donning my best frock to rake dung around, will I! I suggest we get the key to the dairy later and find some old clothes for you too. Then we can both look like Farmer and Mrs Giles.'

I find Elsie already dressed and nursing a pot of tea. 'Bring a cup over,' she says, but doesn't enquire about Gerald.

'I think we can turn the cows out to pasture this morning. Perhaps it's early, but now it's turned milder I think they'll cope. We'll put them in the top fields as they're drier. They'll need hay up there to supplement the grass.'

We head out into the damp air, with a sea breeze at our faces and the dawn lightening up the sky at the horizon. I load the cart with hay, crank up the tractor and head up the farm track.

'Which field Elsie?' I call.

'One on the right, end of the track.'

I heave the bales off the cart and into the hay rack, top up the water trough and stand admiring the sky as it slowly emerges from the night with a band of transparent blue, with crimson tinges appearing on the edges of the fleeing clouds.

By this time Elsie is driving the lumbering cows up the track. As soon as the leading pair spy the open gate, they begin to trot, with the rest of the herd hot on their heels. In spite of their heavy pregnancies they dash as one up to the highest point of the field and back again, out of pure pleasure at being outdoors once more. It's a joyous moment to start the day.

When we return to the yard, we find Gerald and Jack in close conversation in the hay barn while they throw corn for the birds.

'Morning Mrs Dyer,' Gerald calls jovially, 'young Jack here is showing me round the farm, although we've only just got started. He wants to show me the pigs next'.

By the time the porridge is made, they come back pink-cheeked, laughing about the antics of the piglets, and we sit down at the kitchen table like a happy family for breakfast. All the while Gerald keeps up a conversation, mainly with Elsie, asking her all about the farm, giving her something familiar to talk about. I'm proud of his tact and his ability to put her at ease. I think things should run smoothly this weekend, and he and Jack seem to have hit it off together too.

Afterwards we leave Jack to finish showing Gerald around and head to the cow shed to muck it out and spread the dung.

'Your husband seems nice, Helen, and Jack's taken to him.'

That's about the only time she mentions Gerald, but I take it as a positive sign.

Jack.

Mr Day has been to stay for two weekends now. He's fun. Proper fun with games and jokes that make me laugh. I thought he might be like Bert, and I would never know what to say to him, but Mr Day isn't at all like Bert.

I took him all round the farm the first time he was here, and he asked me all sorts of things about it without making fun of me as if I didn't really know what I was talking about. He was interested. He ought to be a teacher. I think he would be good at that.

I'd like to be in his class, anyway.

On the first afternoon he found some old clothes in his case in the dairy and after that he didn't mind getting mucky. He told me he used to visit farms to see sick animals and often he had to go in the middle of the night to help a sheep or a cow have its baby if it was difficult. He told me he sometimes had to put his whole arm inside a cow's bottom to pull the calf out. I thought he was joking at first. That sounds disgusting. I told him I wouldn't want to be a veterinary if I had to do that, but he said if I was going to be a farmer, they sometimes had to do it themselves if the veterinary wasn't there. I'll have to think about that one.

Aunty Helen was really happy to have her husband here, I think. On the first Sunday afternoon it was quite sunny and they went for a long walk together. I wanted to go with them but Mrs Dyer said to me quietly that I should find something else to do and let them have some time together. I watched them walk out the drive hand in hand which looked a bit silly.

Last Sunday, though, I did go for a walk with them. Mrs Dyer always tells us that we should take Sunday afternoons off from working on the farm, but often she goes out to do something anyway, so it was just the three of us. It was fun just being with Aunty Helen and her husband for a while. We climbed a long way up the downs, which I think is a really stupid name because the downs are ups, not downs.

Mr Day had to stop a few times to get his breath back and Aunty Helen kept asking him if he was alright to go on. He was fine when we were at the top and it was flatter. We were very high up and we could look down on the whole of Ventnor town. Out to sea there were a few ships in the distance, but no aeroplanes today. Not far away we could see some tall masts and Aunty Helen told us that they had been hit by the bombs in the two air raids we had. They looked alright to me so someone must have repaired them.

Today, when I return from school, there's a letter for me from Mum. I can read quite well now but Mum's handwriting is awful and I need Aunty Helen to help me.

Dear Jack.

Thank you for the newspaper cutting. It looks like you had some excitement down there. I hope that German got what was coming to him. I bet you were scared. Bert says Mrs Dyer should have shot him there and then.

I turn to Aunty Helen. 'I wasn't really scared, was I? And I don't think the man wanted to hurt us, did he?'
'No, he didn't want to hurt us, he was just a pilot doing what his country told him to do. He was hungry and thirsty and in a lot of pain with his burns so I think he was glad to be captured.'
She carries on with Mum's letter.

It's been very exciting here too. Guess what. You have a new baby sister! She's really gorgeous with black hair like Bert and blue eyes like me. She came earlier than we expected and had to go to the hospital for a few days, but she's fine now and you're going to love her! We're using one of the drawers out of the chest for a cot for her and she sleeps next to the bed. We're going to call her Iris Anne. Do you like that?
The other good news is that Mr Grimshaw who works at Bert's place has agreed to collect you from Portsmouth in the holidays if your folks can arrange for you to get there. He drives down every Wednesday and you'd need to be there by about eleven in the morning. He can take you back the following week. So you know who he is, he'll hold up a paper with your name on and he'll meet you when you come off the ferry. If he isn't there for some reason, just wait where you are in case he's been held up in traffic or something. He's very tall, with dark hair and a big moustache. Can you come on 19th March so you can spend the Easter weekend with us.
Write and let me know when it's arranged.

We'll see you in a few weeks,
Love Mum and Bert, and baby Iris.

I don't know what to think about having a baby sister. I think I'm supposed to be excited and say I'm looking forward to seeing her, but a baby is just a baby and really not very exciting. They usually sleep all day or cry.

'Well, Jack, it looks like you'll be going home at Easter. We'll have to see how we're going to get you to Portsmouth in time.'

I nod. I suppose it will be alright.

Helen

After Jack received his letter he was unusually quiet all evening. I'm not sure he was too enthusiastic about having a baby sister, or perhaps it was the worry about going home.

I spoke to Elsie when Jack was out of earshot and showed her the letter. We both agreed that it was a little presumptuous of Mrs Patton that one of us would convey Jack to Portsmouth, without actually asking us in person. She had not mentioned anything about transport costs from Ventnor to Ryde and then the ferry fare. It seemed to be assumed that we would foot the bill. Of course we would do that, but it would have been courteous to have asked, especially as it will take up a whole working day at a busy time of year.

Apart from all that, it will be strange not having Jack running about all day in the holidays. I hope Mrs Patton doesn't decide he should stay with them for the rest of the war. I suppose it's a possibility.

Today we have the cold and muddy task of planting another field of potatoes. While Simmy and Elsie are both working down the row, I return to the stable to fetch another tray of chits. As I cross the yard a vehicle draws in and two men step out. I recognise them as the men from the Agricultural Committee.

'Good morning,' the senior man doffs his hat.

'Is Mrs Dyer about?'

'Yes, we're potato-planting. I'll take you.'

'You work here full time do you?'

'Yes, I've been here since July. Have you come for another inspection?'

They tell me they have come to see how the farm is progressing after their report of last year.

While I walk with them I give them a glowing report of all the things we've put in practice.

I leave Mrs Dyer to show them around the farm and discuss the details with them, but as I bend again to the back-breaking task of potato-planting I have a thought about Gerald's future.

Before the men return to their car, I accost them in the yard.

'Excuse me. May I ask you a question?'

They both look at me politely.

'Are there many vacancies for farm inspectors at the moment?'

They look at each other, clearly surprised by the question. 'Well, there's a war on and the nation needs the farming community to step up it's production, so I should think there are places that still need inspectors. Why do you ask?'

'My husband is unable to enlist but I think he would be perfectly suited for this kind of job. Where would they be advertised?'

They consult each other. 'We think the first port of call would be the local Agricultural Committees, depending on what area he wants to work. What is his background?'

I don't really want to go into details at the moment so I just tell them that Gerald is a veterinary but finds himself unemployed right now. I ask them what sort of experience is needed and they tell me that men come from various backgrounds related to farming and food production. The younger man consults his clipboard and tears off a sheet of headed paper.

'This is the address of the Island Committee. They may be able to help with addresses of committees in other areas.'

They bid me good day and I pocket the sheet of paper. I hope the idea might inspire Gerald. He hasn't been particularly proactive about job-hunting up till now and he is likely to be discharged before Easter. I head back to the mud and potatoes before I'm accused of shirking.

Friday dawns mild and cloudy and after the morning chores I walk down the road with Jack, he on his way to school and me to carry out my morning's work at Downs Farm.

'How's school, Jack?' I ask.

'It's fine. We've got nature study today and PE. They are both my favourites so I like Fridays. And now your husband comes on Friday evenings and he's fun.'

I'm really pleased Gerald has scored such a hit with Jack, although perhaps I'm just a tiny amount put out that he's usurped my position in the popularity stakes!

'The Easter holiday will be coming up soon, are you looking forward to it?'

He looks at me with a frown. 'I don't really know. '

I give his hand a squeeze.

'I know you're a bit worried about it but it will be an adventure to go somewhere completely new and see Mum again. And you'll be getting a ride in a big lorry too.'

He skips off down the road when we reach my junction and I head up to see Hugh and Molly Taylor.

They are both in the kitchen when I arrive and as I settle down to work, Mr Taylor updates me on orders to place and bills to prioritise. While he is there I ask him,

'Do you know anything about farm inspectors, Mr Taylor, like qualifications or experience they need?'

'I'm not sure if I know very much, why do you ask?'

I explain that Gerald will be discharged soon and will not be able to cope with heavy work such as he sometimes had to do when carrying out veterinary visits. I tell him that we are looking for jobs that he might cope with that still involve outdoor work.

'I should think your husband might be well placed for that sort of job. I don't suppose it involves heavy lifting or anything like that. Have you tried the local Agricultural Committee?'

I tell him that the inspector who visited recently suggested I do that.

Molly Taylor chips in, 'I know from the past, one of the inspectors that came round to us. Probably the same ones as you had. He used to be a manager at the Farmer's Cooperative in Newport.'

'Have you thought about the Milk Marketing Board?' Hugh Taylor asks me.

'The MMB inspectors are out and about all day checking and advising on milk standards. I should think your husband must know a thing or two about that. With this war on, more farms are having to step up their milk production like we are, so there must be a demand for inspectors.'

They give me some advice to think about and things to suggest to Gerald when he comes to stay this weekend. I just hope he is more open to considering his next move.

When I collect him later from the hospital he is in good spirits. He kisses me in greeting.

'I so look forward to this, Helen,' Gerald tells me as we walk out to the horse and dog cart.

We bowl along Undercliff Drive, Biddy seeming to be catching Gerald's high spirits.

'I really like it on the farm. If it wasn't for these wretched lungs of mine, I'd suggest we bought a little property somewhere and had some livestock. I don't think I could cope right now, though, especially in the cold and wet.'

'I've got a couple of other ideas for you that we could talk about later,' I say hopefully as we reach Jack's school to collect him.

After that it's all greetings and talking non-stop about his day in the classroom so I place the ideas on hold for a more opportune time.

CHAPTER 20

SPRING BRINGS CHANGE

Elsie

This morning Elsie is up and out earlier than usual. There's a definite feeling of spring in the air, the promise of a fine day and a dry one too after days of rain churning the track to mud. The cow's are making a mire around their gate too. Only the pigs are happy.

She walks briskly up the track to the top of the farm to check on the cows. It will only be a day or two before they start to calve and there was one yesterday that was hanging around a little distance from the rest. Elsie has a feeling she could give birth today.

Most of the cows are quietly grazing, a few look up curiously as she wades through the gateway and sure enough, there by the hedge is the first birth. Elsie can see it has only just happened. The young calf is lying on the ground still wet and slimy as the mother licks it clean and nudges it. Elsie grabs a handful of rough grass and rubs the infant, poking her finger into its mouth to clear any obstruction. The mother nudges it hard to stand up, and on wobbly legs it butts the cow until it's mouth latches onto the udder. It's a male and drinks greedily.

Elsie scans round the rest of the herd. None of the other girls seem imminent just yet, so she finishes the rest of the morning chores and returns to the kitchen. Jack will be thrilled with this news and after breakfast she decides to take him on the tractor to see the newborn before he has to leave for school.

Helen elects to come too before she has to catch the bus to Wroxall and the two of them perch at the back of the tractor whooping and shouting as they bounce over the potholes.

They watch the first of the year young calf as it drunkenly tries out it's gangly legs, gathering strength by the minute until it flops into the grass and curls up as if the effort has exhausted it.

'Can I stroke it?' asks Jack, but Elsie suggests they leave mother and calf in peace for now but that he'll have an opportunity after school to help her bring both of them down to a nearer field. She scans around the herd once more and reckons more births are imminent.

Later, as she works alongside Simmy, she considers the changes about to take place on the farm. Firstly, it's now the start of the milking season, meaning earlier mornings and more work. Secondly, Mr Day will be discharged from hospital in a couple of days, providing his last assessment goes well. He seems quite robust, a little breathless with exertion, but otherwise fit and healthy, so she assumes all will be well.

At Helen's suggestion, they did make contact with the Agriculture Committee and the Ministry of Food, enquiring about job vacancies, but she doesn't know if anything has come of that. If he finds a job elsewhere, she will lose Helen and that will leave her with another headache, just when the busiest season is about to start.

She was very anxious about having a man about the place these last few weekends and feared Mr Day may be the sort of person to hand out endless unwanted advice about running a farm. She's had enough of that from the Ministry Men and her husband. Her worries were unfounded, though. She found he always had something to chat about with her so she wasn't left feeling uncomfortable and lost for something to say. He was eager to learn about the farm and happy to get his hands dirty as long as he didn't have to do anything too strenuous. He was marvelous with Jack too. The more Elsie thinks about it, she realises she's enjoyed the weekends he was here, much to her surprise.

Also, when Helen and Mr Day leave, Elsie realises she will have to consider Jack. Helen has really taken over his care since the start, which is time consuming in itself. She can't really bring herself to ask for him to be rehoused. Not after all this time. Perhaps Mrs Patton will keep him in Jaywick, she thinks, with mixed feelings about it.

When Jack returns from school she gathers him and Helen to help her move the new cow and calf.

They hitch up the small cart with the cage around it to the tractor and she drives while Helen and Jack stand on the back.

At the field they approach the calf who is now gambolling about discovering his new legs and she positions herself and Helen to either side of it. Without alarming the little fellow, one of them needs to gather him up and carry him to the cart. With practiced efficiency Elsie manages to scoop him up and accompanied by concerned mooing from the mother, she carries him out to the waiting tractor.

'Are you taking it away from its mother?' Jack asks worriedly.

'No, don't worry, let her follow us out of the gate and then shut it behind us. She'll follow the cart'.

They ride back on the tractor, calf bawling at his mother, while she keeps close behind, following us to the small field near the cowshed. The calf leaps out the cart when Helen opens the catch and immediately runs to the mother for a comfort suckle. Both are content once again.

'We can keep an eye on the new ones better in here. After they've had some time together we'll start milking, and bring the calves a pail of the milk twice a day. I think you can help with that Jack. You might run up to the top field each morning too, and see if there are any more calves for me to check on.'

He hops up and down. He was hoping he might help with the calves.

Helen

With the lighter evenings I've been able to visit Gerald late in the afternoons on Wednesdays and Sundays so that I can spend most of the day on the farm where it's been especially busy. We had three more new calves at the weekend, although none so far this week. Jack is thrilled to be in charge of bringing the news each morning. I believe it was a useful idea of Elsie's to give Jack another morning task while we are out at the milking shed and give him exercise running up and down the track.

Elsie has been slightly preoccupied for a few days. She had another letter from her husband asking her to visit again.

'I knew this would happen,' she confided with me when Jack was at school.

'I imagine he wants more money, but he'll have to whistle for that. I think he's lost touch with what everyone is coping with in the outside world, and I haven't the time to keep running off to visit him every five minutes. I shall tell him that when I see him.'

I request the visiting forms again for her and send them back to the prison.

Today Gerald has been having his final assessment and x-ray and if all is well he will be discharged on Friday. I walk briskly along the Undercliff Drive to the hospital. I suspect that he has been procrastinating about finding a new job until he has been given the all clear. It is all quite unsettling, though, not knowing where we are going from the weekend on. I'm sure Mrs Dyer will not ask us to leave just yet, but we soon need to start recouping our savings, part of which has gone to pay the hospital bills, although my two mornings work will at least pay for Gerald's lodgings plus a little extra.

Gerald was finally motivated enough to make some enquiries about jobs but we are yet to hear anything and really he needs to follow this up.

I enter the wide gates of the hospital, continually in awe of the majestic facade stretching so far along the front of the grounds, certainly an impressive piece of architecture, housing an equally impressive sanatorium.

I make my way to the communal lounge. Gerald is not there but another gentleman that I've seen many times says,

'He's in his room, dear. Shame he'll be leaving us soon, I like your young man.'

I find Gerald reclining fully-clothed on the bed and immediately feel concern that his assessment may not have gone well.

'Hello, love. How are you?' I sit on the bed.

He folds the newspaper he's been reading.

'I'm fine, darling. Just having a rest. I've had about four professionals of one sort or another pushing and pummeling me, checking my breathing, my lung function, strength, stamina, you name it! It's all good, though. The x-ray showed up some scarring, only to be expected, but slightly more than the consultant hoped for. He still considered me well enough to go home, though. How about that!'

We give ourselves a celebratory hug.

'Marvelous news, my love.' I tell him, and it certainly is.

'I had a very long lecture afterwards from Matron about what I can or can't do at the moment. Don't worry,' he says with a cheeky twinkle in his eye, 'that's quite allowed as long as it doesn't involve any swinging chandeliers!'

'Gerald!'

He shows me several sheets of headed paper with a list of all the guidelines the matron outlined, a schedule of future check-ups and various guidelines about things to avoid, breathing exercises to do regularly and guidance on keeping a healthy diet. The hospital is nothing but comprehensive in its care for patients.

'I can be released on Friday when they have all my medical notes up together and the final assessment information in case I have to visit a doctor for anything. I can't wait, Helen.'

I want to address the issue of our future but right now I'm reluctant to spoil his euphoria. It must feel like he's walking on air after all this time to have the prospect of home in a couple of days. Although I don't know if he's given much thought to what is 'home'.

I walk back to the farm slowly, enjoying the mild evening with peach and pink shades infusing the sky above the clouds hovering over the horizon. It feels strange to think that things will change for me in two days time. I have settled into the routines of nature on the farm, my body has grown into the hard work, the cold of the winter and the early mornings. I am content with our trio living on the farm, and the quiet corner (or relative quiet) of this island, away from the real atrocities of the war being experienced by so many people in the cities. Much as I'm looking forward to the return of Gerald, it will change things and that, at the moment, is the great unknown.

Jack

I'm excited walking home from school. This is the day that Aunty Helen is collecting her husband from the hospital for the last time. I think he'll be home when I get there. I'm looking forward to him being on the farm for now, even though Aunty Helen keeps telling me that they will have to move away soon. I don't want to think about that just yet because he's fun and I like doing all the jobs with him. I've never had a Dad and he's like a Dad should be. I can't think of Bert as a Dad because he isn't really interested in me. I think he finds me a nuisance. My Mum said I should call him Uncle Bert when he started to come round to the house most days, but I didn't want to. I tried to avoid calling him anything at all! I would like to call Mr Day Uncle, but I don't think I can ask him yet. Anyway, it makes me skip down the lane to the farm, watching the birds flitting everywhere in the hedgerow. They are really busy now it's spring.

We have three new calves now and Mrs Dyer thinks there will be more this weekend. They are so cute and lively and soon I can help when they get the pails of milk each day. It's annoying that I have to go to Jaywick next week just when there's lots of good things to do on the farm and now Mr Day will be here too. It's not fair.

In the morning Mr Day walks up the track with me to see the cows while Mrs Dyer, Helen and Simmy do the milking. They only have a few cows that are ready yet, so it won't take them long.

It's quite breezy up here today but the sun is up and the sea is sparkling so it's going to be another fine day.

Mr Day whistles as we walk and I try to whistle as well, but nothing comes out. He tries to show me how to put my tongue and lips, but I still just blow out air without any sound. He says we can practice and soon I'll get it.

We open the field gate and scan the field for calves.

'I can see three calves, Jack.' Mr Day points to the nearest one. 'This little fellow has just been born, look.'

We stand over the new calf and Mr Day rubs it with a clump of grass, just like Mrs Dyer did on the first day.

I'm getting used to seeing all this mucky, slimy and bloody stuff come out of the cow's bottom afterwards, although the first time it made me squeal and wrinkle my nose up. I thought there was something wrong with the cow. Mrs Dyer told me it was the afterbirth and just the stuff that the calf was growing inside. It all sounds pretty disgusting to me but Mrs Dyer said it was the same with all animals, including humans. I think she might have been joking about the last bit. I tell Mr Dyer it's just the after-birth in case it makes him feel a bit sick, but he reminds me that he was a veterinary and has often seen it.

'Are you going to be a veterinary again?' I ask him.

'Not at the moment son. My lungs aren't good enough. Some-times when you're a vet you have to do some strenuous things like lifting sheep and flipping them onto their backs to examine them or give them medicine. We might have to push big heavy horses around to look at their hooves or carry sick calves from a field to a shed. All sorts of unexpected things can crop up.'

We leave the mother and calf in peace and look around at the others.

'That one's got a white circle round one eye.' I point out a wobbly legged calf staring at us curiously.

'She ought to be called Patch.'

I like that name. It's a good idea and it's a girl calf so she should be staying on the farm till she's grown up. Mrs Dyer says the boy calves have to be sold because she can only keep ones that produce milk.

The other calf that must have been born since we last came up here is jumping around with two of yesterday's calves. It's a boy.

We head back to the farm for breakfast and I skip along beside Mr Dyer. He tries to skip along with me, but he's not terribly good at it and after a while he gets out of breath so has to walk again. I like being with him, though.

Helen

This week with Gerald has flown by. There's much to do and more cows to start milking each day. The piglets are growing enormous and need so much feed. I still collect the pig swill but I've added two more pick-up points so need to take an extra bin with me. Gerald is loving it here and has volunteered to help with the milking. He's pretty good at it and faster than me, so I'm now in charge of the milk pails for the calves. Once the calves have been with their mothers a few days we bring them into the cow shed. Of course that creates a good deal of bawling from the cows, becoming separated for the first time, but they soon get used to it.

Jack loves helping me and lets the calves suck milk from his fingers until they learn to put their mouths round the rubber teats.

On Sunday afternoon Gerald and I go with Jack for a long walk. Mrs Dyer, as usual, spends her afternoon off still doing odd jobs around the farm!

Since I've been working here, I haven't really explored my surroundings much. Partly it's because there's always something else we should do, but also because it feels a little awkward walking far alone. It's a real treat to all go out together and we find our way along the trail leading along the cliff top towards St Lawrence. It's really high up and offers stunning views across Ventnor to the sea, especially as it's a lovely afternoon of sunshine. We stand looking down over the huge Royal Chest Hospital which has been Gerald's home for the last eight months and we point it out to Jack who is quite amazed at the size of it.

'Gosh, it does give you a good birds eye view of it up here, doesn't it?' Gerald takes a long look, working out all the places he worked in the grounds. He never had a real feel for the size of the place while he was in it, especially as half of it is the women's side, separated by a wall from the male side.

He's so enjoying the farm and wants to get stuck into all sorts of jobs. At night he whispers to me about all the things he would do if it was his, but at least has the good sense not to mention them to Mrs Dyer! Of course, he cannot cope with all the jobs we do each day. Hefting bales of hay is not a job for him, but he can muck out the pigsty and the stable as long as he takes it steadily. He's enjoying his new found freedom so much that he keeps procrastinating about finding a job. I just have to be patient I suppose before I become even more of a nag.

Jack is loving it up on the cliff top. He runs on ahead, finds trees he wants to climb and then comes between us so we can swing him up as we walk. We wind our way down the footpaths to the Undercliff Drive and then down again and more steep steps until we find ourselves in Steephill Cove, a pretty little fishing cove bounded by rocks, enclosing a golden shingle and sand beach. Small fishing boats are pulled up beyond the surf and stacks of lobster pots line the beach. A couple of pretty thatched cottages look out onto the cove along with a more modern building and several wooden fishing shacks.

A few families are enjoying their Sunday time off and two brave children are paddling in the shallow waves. 'Can I paddle?' Jack looks expectantly at us both.

I look at Gerald and he gives the faintest of shrugs so we help the lad pull off his socks and shoes and in he goes, his shorts immediately soaked way above the hems. He runs in and out with the surf, laughing and calling.

'It's freezing, you know!'

'We do know,' says Gerald. 'That's why we're standing here in the warm!'

Eventually we drag him out, legs almost purple and encourage him to run up and down on the shingle until he's dry enough to pull the socks back on.

It must all be such a far cry from his London upbringing. I wonder how he's going to cope next week in Jaywick, seeing his mother and a new baby. At least it will be near the sea, not the middle of a huge council estate under threat of the bombs.

I can see he's quite anxious about his visit and we'll be leaving tomorrow morning to get him to the ferry in time to catch his lift from Portsmouth. It will be a long day for him.

Jack.

I curl up under some blankets on the sofa in the lounge. I wanted to go to sleep ages ago, I'm so tired, but Mum was still sitting on the sofa and Bert was in the chair listening to a play on the radio. I had to wait till their bedtime before they brought the blankets in for me.

It's been a really long day. Aunty Helen took me on the train this morning before I caught the ferry. She asked the ferry lady to look after me till I got to Portsmouth. I felt really scared in case that Mr Grimshaw wasn't there to meet me, but he was. He held up a piece of paper with my name on it, so I knew it was him.

He was quite friendly and helped me climb up into his lorry and it was great fun sitting up so high looking down on the other cars and vans on the road. We met loads of army lorries on the way and even a group of tanks trundling their way on the other side of the road.

It took ages and ages and we only stopped twice, once for Mr

Grimshaw to fill the lorry up with fuel and then again in a lay-by for us both to go behind the hedge for a pee. Aunty Helen made me some sandwiches and we had our lunch there too.

When we reached Clacton Mr Grimshaw had to park the lorry back at his factory and then I rode on the back of his motorbike to Jaywick where he dropped me off. It's the first time I've ever been on a motorbike which was fun, but really cold and I was frozen when I arrived at Mum's place.

'Hello Son,' she said, when I walked into the sittingroom, 'you made it then.'

She was holding the baby in her arms.

'Here, what do you think of your new baby sister, then?'

I hadn't even put my bag down or taken my coat off when she thrust the bundle at me and said,

'Give her a cuddle.'

I had to drop my things on the floor and hold this baby, without dropping her, so I sat on the settee in case she wriggled out my arms. She didn't do anything, just stared at my face with big round blue eyes. I suppose she's cute, but all babies are cute.

Bert wasn't around at that time but he came in soon after when Mum was cooking tea.

'Ah, here's our young Farmer Jack, then. Brought yer pig, have yer?' He laughed at his joke, but there's not much to say to that really.

'Seen our pretty little Iris, have you?'

'Yes,' I tell him. 'I held her.'

Mum put the baby in the pram, a huge great black and shiny thing that takes up half the space in the room, and rocked her till she fell asleep. She parked the pram beside the table at one side of the kitchen and we all had to squash round it to eat our fish fingers and beans. Mum kept rocking the pram and fiddling with the bedcover and it was Bert who asked me lots of questions about the farm. Things like how many cows are there, how are they milked, why haven't they got a milking machine, what sort of tractor is it, what breed of pigs has Mrs Dyer got, and finally, where is her husband. So many things I didn't know and I began to feel stupid, but Bert always does that when I'm around. I was glad when it was bedtime because I was nearly asleep all evening.

I feel cold this morning when I wake. I pull the blankets up tight and curl up but it's difficult to keep the cold out. I can hear the wind howling outside and as the front door leads straight into the sitting room, the wind whistles under the crack and nearly sliced my ankles off all last evening.

I can hear voices and movements through the thin wall to the bedroom and soon Bert comes through the sitting room. I hear him go outside, presumably to the toilet in the yard and then he clatters around in the small kitchen at the back. I keep my head down low and pretend to still be asleep.

'Want a brew, Jack?' he shouts to me. So he knows I'm awake. I go into the kitchen in my pyjamas and accept a cup of tea which is really dark brown and strong. Bert grabs a piece of toast that he's making and crams it into his mouth as he throws his jacket on and heads off to work. I pour my tea down the sink.

I dress in yesterday's clothes, put my best Christmas jumper on as well to keep warm and venture out to the yard. The sky is full of grey rushing clouds and perhaps it will even rain later, I think. I sit at one end of the table with Mum nursing the baby at the other end.

'So, tell me about this 'Aunty Helen', you talk about,' she says to me. The way she says Aunty Helen's name, makes me think she doesn't like her, but she's never met her.

I tell her she's really nice and used to take me to school. I tell her about Mr Day and how he has been very ill, but now he's staying on the farm for a while.

'I don't think you should be staying in the same house as someone with tuberculosis,' she says rather primly.

'He's quite well now, Mum. He doesn't have it anymore.'

I tell her about the pigs and the new calves being born every day this last week. I describe the calves and how I help with their milking pails in the morning, but I don't think she's listening anymore, she's fussing with that wretched baby. I eat my toast.

As we clear the table she plucks at my jumper and says, 'I suppose 'Aunty Helen' knitted you that.'

She uses that sarcastic voice again.

'Actually,' I say, 'it was Mrs Dyer who knitted it for me out of one of her husband's old jumpers. It's nice and warm.'

'And where is this husband of Mrs Dyer's, you never told us.'

'I think he's abroad doing something secret for the war.'

Later we walk out, with Mum pushing the giant pram to 'give Iris some air'.

We walk down our unmade lane that has a row of holiday cabins down one side and scrubby sand on the other side that slopes gradually to a browny-grey sea in the distance. It's all very flat, not like the isle of Wight.

The holiday places are all different sizes. A few are quite smart, with a coat of coloured paint, but most of them are quite scruffy with peeling paint and lots of weeds growing in front. They are mostly wooden and some have been patched up with planks and bits of metal. There's one that's just an old caravan with a garden shed tacked to it. The one Mum's staying in is unpainted wooden boards with a flat roof. The window frames were painted white once but they are going quite rotten now, which is probably why it's so damp inside. Mum says it's because of the paraffin heaters. She mops up the pools of condensation off the windowsills every morning with an old towel.

She was right about it being small. The front room is just big enough for the sofa and an arm chair, and the sideboard on one wall, plus the ridiculous pram. Their bedroom leads off the sitting room and that's a bit of a squash too with a drawer propped onto a kitchen chair next to the bed for Iris to sleep in.

The kitchen is at the back and doesn't get any sun so there's black mould spots creeping up the corners onto the ceiling. I suppose it's better than being bombed in London, but I don't like it very much.

The wind is blasting off the sea, blowing a layer of sand into the potholes. I wish I had long trousers on and that old coat of Mr Dyer's that I wear around the farm. My school mackintosh isn't thick enough but Aunty Helen thought I should look smart to come here. I pull my scarf up over my nose. If Iris needed some air, Mum could have parked her in the yard without us having to go through this, I think.

In the afternoon, I feel bored.

'What can I do, Mum?'

She tells me there's some cards in the sideboard drawer if I want to play pairs or patience. There's also a jigsaw puzzle but it has five hundred pieces so I don't think I can do it.

I play cards for a while and in the end I read one of the story books that Aunty Helen bought me even though I've read it loads of times now. I wonder what we're going to do all week.

It's Saturday before we do anything different. I haven't seen the sunshine yet, but there's a glimmer of brightness over the sea, so perhaps it won't be quite so gloomy today.

Mum and I walk along the coast into Clacton, Mum pushing the pram, of course. She has a few bits of shopping to do so we head to the High Street. It's much bigger than Ventnor with quite a lot of shops. There are queues here too, and a few soldiers hanging around in groups. They look bored as well. Mum buys some vegetables, and dried milk and egg from the grocer that she has to give her ration coupons for.

'Can I have a comic, Mum,' I ask hopefully.

'As you're on holiday, I suppose so,' she says and we find a newsagent and I choose a comic I haven't tried before. I tell Mum it's a new one I haven't seen yet.

'I suppose 'Aunty Helen' buys you the comics,' she says, using that voice again. I think Mum is quite jealous that Aunty Helen sees more of me than she does, but Mum's the one who sent me to the Isle of Wight in the first place.

I just nod. At least I'll have something to read this evening.

By the time we arrive back at the cabin, Bert is home from work. He only works half a day on Saturday. He has his feet up on a footstool and reads the paper.

'Are we getting any lunch today?' he asks grumpily.

'It's only just twelve, Bert. Give me ten minutes.'

Mum hurriedly discards her overcoat and ties herself into her pinafore, rushing about in the kitchen.

'Can I help, Mum?' I ask her, trying to be useful, but also aiming for an excuse to stay in the kitchen so I don't have to talk to Bert.

'No, son. You'll just be in the way. Go in there and talk to Bert while I get this lunch cooked.'

I wander back in the sitting room trying to think of things to say, when Iris lets out a huge wail and starts bawling her eyes out.

'Rock the baby, Jack,' Mum shouts.

I rock the pram hard but she won't shut up.

'For Christ sake!' Bert shakes his paper aggressively, 'pick the kid up and rock her.'

I want to ask why he can't do it, but I'm not brave enough so I grab hold of my sister and jump her up and down. She carries on wailing and getting on my nerves now.

'Oh, for goodness sake,' Mum snatches her off me. 'Go and have your lunch, both of you, it's on the table.' She stomps off to the bedroom with Iris.

I sit down with Bert and pick at my corned beef hash, wishing that Wednesday would hurry up and come.

Elsie

Elsie sits down on the hard chair facing Arthur across the small table. She is not in the best of moods as this visit is taking up the best part of her day when she has better things to do. At least Gerald is is on the farm now, she thinks, and can take over the evening milking. He's actually a welcome addition to the farm in her opinion even with the limit of things he can easily do. She's not in a hurry to see them leave, even though Helen tends to nag him about his future career. They understandably want to carve a new life for themselves, but she has no need to ask them to leave.

She sits primly, brown leather handbag tightly clasped in her lap and waits for Arthur to speak first.

'Nice of you to come, Else. Shame I had to ask,' he adds sarcastically.

'I'm busy, Arthur. This takes most of my day to come here so I can't be turning up every five minutes to bring you bread pudding.'

She hands over the wedge of pudding wrapped in greaseproof paper.

'That's not all I want, Else. I could do with more money for one thing.'

Elsie stares at him grimly.

'Not a chance. We're only just making ends meet. We've only been milking a couple of weeks and the piglets aren't ready yet.'

'Well I want you to sell the farm, Else.'

'What?' Elsie wasn't sure she'd heard correctly.

'Sell the farm. I'll settle a decent share for you.'

'What do you mean, you'll settle me with a share? I'm running the damn farm now.'

Arthur stares her down.

'Farm's in my name. I want it sold.'

'Have you forgotten there's a war on? No one wants to buy farms at the moment and labour's hard to find. You'd be lucky to give it away and if I wasn't there just about making it pay for itself, you'd have the Ministry requisitioning it.'

Elsie sets her face with a determined expression even though her heart has started to race with frustration and anger.

'You won't know till you've put it on the market, will you?'

Elsie can hear that he's starting to get stroppy with her.

'Look, Arthur, like I say, it will be really difficult to sell now and we'd have to take such a loss on it even if there was such a buyer. Why don't we hang on until the war's over. There'll be hundreds of troops returning home with men wanting to make a new start. The price of farms will surely rise.'

'All very well, but I don't see no signs of the war ending yet, do you?'

'It's not going to carry on for ever and you're not going anywhere just yet, are you, so you might as well be patient and reap a profit instead of giving it away.'

'I see, rub it in, why don't you.'

Elsie is feeling braver now.

'It's my last word on it, Arthur. We'll discuss it again when the war's over.'

She pushes her chair back and nods to the officer at the door. She looks back at her husband.

'Take care of yourself.'

She walks out smartly, letting out a long breath.

As she waits for the bus outside, she realises her hands are still shaking. It's always been difficult for her to stand her ground against Arthur.

Unfortunately Arthur could probably set the wheels in motion himself to have the farm sold. It's still in his name. She hopes he now sees the sense of waiting but it wouldn't hurt for her to seek some legal advice. Not that she can afford it, she reminds herself ruefully. Hopefully she's bought herself some time as goodness knows what she'd do if she sold the farm. It's her whole life. She'll have to think of a contingency plan just in case.

Helen.

None of us seem to be talking about the future. It's like the war is keeping everyone and everything on hold until it's over, although that sounds like it could still be a long way off. The Germans continue their relentless blitz of British cities with terrible loss of life and homes reduced to rubble or engulfed in flames. Coventry, Manchester, Hull, Plymouth, Southampton, Liverpool, all targeted and of course, London which has been bombed night after night. There have been a few times when we've heeded the air raid sirens, heard great swarms of bombers winging their way in formation low over the channel, and run to the shelter. We've cowered there in the candlelight listening to the engines droning overhead towards their deadly mission on the south coast. The anti aircraft guns boom in response, the sound reverberating through the ground.

After these disturbed and uncomfortable nights we always feel subdued listening to the news and thank God for the good fortune of living on the Island and give silent prayers for all the unlucky people caught in the path of those deadly raids.

I've stopped thinking (and nagging) about our future. It's too difficult for any of us to think about finding new jobs, buying new houses or moving to places that may be less safe while the war still rages on, so, without any discussion we just carry on with the status quo.

Even Elsie, who came home spitting feathers from the prison after her husband told her to sell the farm, has shrugged her shoulders and decided to do nothing. 'Dreadful place!' she declared after returning from the prison visit. 'I shan't be visiting again in a hurry. He'll have to wait for his money. It will be madness trying to sell the farm now, even if I wanted to, which I don't. He seems to think he might be pardoned at the end of the war, but that's just a stupid pipe dream. I reckon it'll be ten years at least before he gets parole'.

This afternoon the bus winds its way out of Ventnor towards Ryde. I sit on the front seat watching the countryside slide past below me. I chose not to take the train today as I thought the bus would be a pleasant way to enjoy a sightseeing tour of the Island. I'm collecting Jack from the ferry and I wonder what sort of week he's had at home. It's a pity the weather wasn't better for his holiday. It's been grey and showery with a chilly wind, temperatures on the low side for the time of year. We could do with a stretch of sunny weather to encourage the crops.

I arrive at the terminal and find a bench to wait on, looking out on The Solent so I can see when the paddle steamer is on her way.

I watch as Jack walks off the ferry clutching his bag. He sees me and comes running, a broad smile lighting up his face. He flings himself at me and I give him a huge hug. It feels the most natural thing in the world and I choke back a tear of emotion. I take his hand and we walk to the station.

'Did you have a good week?'

He shrugs. 'It was a bit boring.'

'What did you think of your baby sister, then.'

'She's okay, I suppose. She's cute but she looks like all babies. She cries really loudly and Bert gets annoyed when she does.'

'Did you tell your Mum all about your adventures on the farm?'

Jack just nods.

I have the feeling he didn't especially enjoy his week away and decide not to ask anymore questions and wait for him to talk about it in his own time if he feels like it.

On the bus he says to me,

'Aunty Helen, I don't really want to go to Jaywick again. Will I have to ?'

'Em, I don't know, Jack. It's not really up to me. If the war goes on a long time, I'm sure your Mum will like to see you again.'

'I'd rather stay on the farm.'

'Well, don't worry about it now. There won't be any more trips for a while. When we get back there's a small surprise for you.'

'What is it?'

I laugh.

'It wouldn't be a surprise if I told you, would it!'

Back at the farm I help him unpack and change into his long trousers. It's still quite chilly, although I was pleased to hear that the weatherman forecast some better temperatures and sunshine after tomorrow.

'Have you had any lunch, Jack?'

'Mr Grimshaw gave me one of his Spam sandwiches when we stopped.'

I can't help tutting. That mother of his sounds pretty useless. Surely she could have sent him with something to eat.

'What's the surprise, Aunty Helen?'

'Come with me now and see, and then we'll come back for something to eat.'

We head to the pig's fields.

'What names did you call the newer pigs, Jack?'

'Flossy and Bossy.'

'Bossy?'

'Yes, she's always bossing the other one around. She's the one with the black patch on her nose.'

We lean over the fence and peer into the corrugated pigsty that Simmy put together.

'Oh, she's had babies!' he squeals.

'Is that Bossy or Flossy?'

'I think it's Flossy.'

'We can go in and have a closer look.' We push open the gate and squelch through the mud to the sty to take a close look at the ten tiny pink piglets, most of them lying asleep in the straw with full stomachs, Flossy lying on her side with a satisfied expression on her face.

'I expect Bossy will have some very soon too. There's plenty of work to keep us all busy.'

Jack wants to know where Gerald is so we follow the sound of banging and find Elsie and Gerald repairing the planks at the side of the hay barn.

'Hello young man.'

Gerald gives him a quick hug.

'Did you have a good week?'

Jack mumbles that it was alright and Elsie gives me a questioning look. I think we both have the same opinion of Mrs Patton.

Jack just wants to talk about the farm and who's been feeding the hens and pigs while he's been away. He takes his jobs very seriously.

I take him back to the farmhouse to find him something to eat and he skips all the way. I can see he's thrilled to be back, as we all are to have him.

CHAPTER 21

JUNE 1965

Jack

What a week to choose for a holiday. Sunshine forecast every day without being burning hot.

Mavis has never been to the Island and it's twenty years since I left here.

After our dinner at the guest house we decide to take a stroll along the promenade towards Bonchurch, enjoying the early evening throng of holiday makers, some still catching the late sunshine on the beaches or enjoying an ice cream on one of the many benches along the way.

The sea is a patchwork of several blues, the white clouds casting deep ultramarine shadows on the water, aqua green shades over the shallows as they wash gently over the sands, silver sparkles further out as the sun sinks lower. Seagulls wheel overhead, some pacing up and down the walkway impatiently waiting for a dropped ice cream or other crumb.

'We ought to be heading back, Jack,' Mavis prompts me. 'We need to be at the theatre for 7.30.'

We've treated ourselves to two tickets for Johnny Kid and the Pirates at The Winter Gardens this evening so we turn around and walk back towards the town.

'The last time I set foot in The Winter Gardens I was five years old. I remember how scared I was, and then I was taken to Mrs Dyer's farm all on my own and nearly cried because she didn't seem very friendly.'

'Fancy your Mum sending you all this way at that age, and not even knowing where you were going to stay.'

She's right. It did seem quite callous, but things worked out for the better in the end. I was lucky to live on the farm, once I'd settled in, and after Helen came.

'Did you stay on the Island for the whole of the war?'

'Yes, I was nearly eleven by the time I left.'

We reach the Winter Gardens where there is already quite a throng of people gathering. It's going to be a popular evening. I tell her that we'll go sightseeing around the Island tomorrow and I'll also show her where Warren farm was. We'll have a few things to talk about by then.

The following day we walk up the hill to Upper Ventnor. It's still just as steep as I remember it, and I point out to Mavis the lane leading to the old RAF station, telling her about the bombing raids and getting caught in the town.

'Goodness, Jack, you were supposed to be here to escape the bombs! Were you hurt?'

'I had a nasty gash on the head, but I was quite proud of my war injury at the time. I could boast about it at school and sported quite a large padded dressing on it. I suppose these days it might have required a stitch or two, but back then it was minor compared with what some people were suffering.' I show Mavis the scar I still have just on my hairline.

We walk on up the lane to the farm and stop at the drive. There's a name plate at the side of the track saying Jackson's Farm. I can see the familiar roof of the farmhouse, but there is nothing except the nameplate to suggest it has changed much.

I tell Mavis a little about our lives on the farm, including the incident with the German airman.

'I've still got the article that was in the local press at home, Mavis. I'll show you when we get back.'

'Did your Mum know about that, Jack?'

I laugh.

'No, I never told her. I was afraid she might want me to go and live in that awful place at Jaywick, but I wanted to stay on the farm.'

After we return to the town and have a morning coffee in one of the several quaint tea and coffee shops, we board the Round The Island Sightseeing Bus.

We manage to bag an upstairs seat so that we have a birds eye view, and this is a treat for me as well because there was little opportunity for sightseeing during the war. I have such a good feeling for the Island that I hope this trip confirms it, and that Mavis is also suitably impressed.

The bus takes us eastwards all along the south coast through the seaside towns of Shanklin and Sandown with it's huge sandy beaches, and then on to Ryde where we hop off for a break before the next bus. Here the tide goes out so far we could almost think it reaches the mainland.

I queue up at a seafood kiosk and buy Mavis a pot of prawns and me a pot of cockles which we eat on a bench looking out towards the pier. Afterwards we walk to the end of the pier and watch the paddle steamer coming in.

Our second bus winds its way north past the entrance to the famous Osborne House and on through the wild west Wight with rolling downs and pretty thatched villages. At the far west where the Needles march off the furthest point of the island, the bus heads back towards Ventnor along the cliff road high above the ocean, with stunning views both right and left.

I needn't have worried that we wouldn't be impressed. As we stroll back to our guest house afterwards Mavis is full of enthusiasm.

'It's really lovely here, isn't it, Jack? It was a good idea of yours to have a week here'.

Over dinner this evening I spring my surprise on her.

'I hoped you'd take to the Island, Mavis because I have a proposition.'

She looks warily at me.

'In the Farmer's weekly there's an advertisement for a Farm Inspector for the Dairy Farmer's Association on the Island. I think I have the right sort of qualifications and experience, and it's offering a little more than I'm earning now. What would you think about me applying?'

'Well...,' Mavis seems lost for words for a second, 'It's a big step, Jack.'

I wait pensively while she mulls it over for a moment.

'You should go for it. I always think if opportunities come your way, you should take them. If you get the job, it's obviously meant for you!'

I take her face in my hands and give her a huge kiss, right there in the dining room, causing two disaproving looks from the couple on the next table.

Mavis takes my hand and laughs.

'If we move down here it will give me an excuse to leave that stuffy old antique centre!'

Over our cups of tea in the garden of the guest house, I suggest something else that I haven't broached with Mavis yet.

'If it's alright with you, I'd like us to pay someone a visit tomorrow, Mavis. I took the liberty of contacting Mrs Dyer who used to own the farm, to see if we could drop in while we're here. Helen still keeps in contact with her from time to time so I know she sold the farm and bought a piece of land at St Lawrence. She had plans to start her tree nursery again, like she and her father had before she married. I got the address from Helen and made contact with her. You don't mind, do you?'

'No. I'd like to meet her. I can ask her what a little nuisance you were as a child!' she says cheekily.

The following day Mavis and I walk along The Undercliff towards St Lawrence. We pass the Royal Chest Hospital where Gerald spent so many months, but it looks closed up now although it's still a very impressive building.

'Goodness, there must have been hundreds of patients. Was there really so much tuberculosis in those days?'

'I suppose there must have been to warrant such a vast building.' It's over two miles before we find the driveway to the tree nursery and Mavis is pleased she wore her slacks and flat shoes.

We see Mrs Dyer watering a row of saplings. She straightens up as we approach, brushing back her hair which is now totally grey and possibly even more unkempt than I remember. She still wears workmanlike trousers and a baggy blue shirt, but raises a dirty hand as we approach and her face lights up.

'Well, I still recognise you, Jack. That's something!'

I introduce her to Mavis and she waves us to the little back garden to sit at the garden chairs in the shade.

'Tea or something cold?'

We both opt for cold and she disappears into her little bungalow, presently joining us with a huge glass jug of fresh lemonade and half a fruit cake.

'I remembered you like the fruit cake, Jack.'

She busies herself pouring drinks and cutting slices of cake and I immediately recognise how she often felt uncomfortable making conversation. At least, with twenty years more experience I can make it easier for her and start by asking her about the nursery.

'I'll show you around after we've had drinks,' she says. 'I'm putting it on the market soon. It's time I retired and I've got my eye on a little place in Bonchurch with an easy garden. I'm not as nimble as I was. Thought I might get myself a little dog for company too.'

She takes a sip of her drink.

'So, what are you two doing at the moment, and where are you living?'

I explain that I gained a degree in agriculture and work as an adviser for a Sussex farming cooperative near Lewes where we have a small flat. Mavis had been living at home working for her parents in their apple orchard when we met, but since we married she's taken an administrative job in an antique centre.

'It doesn't really suit you, though, does it, Honey?' I say to Mavis.

'No. I'm an outdoor person really, like you Mrs Dyer, but it helps pay the mortgage.'

'You can't beat the outdoors, can you, Jack.' Mrs Dyer refills my glass of lemon.

'You really loved being on the farm, didn't you? I felt very sorry for you when you finally went home. You kicked up such a fuss.'

'I can imagine he did,' says Mavis.

She's met my mother and Bert so she has a pretty good idea how I felt.

I reflect back on my relationship with Mum during that time which deteriorated each time I visited. Each year of the war I made the trip to Jaywick during the Easter holidays but managed to avoid going any more often than that.

I was insanely jealous of Iris because of all the attention that was given to her, and Mum only had eyes for her. I felt I was in the way all the time, left out of her affections, feeling bored and resentful because I was missing all the activity on the farm.

About mid way through 1944 Mum wrote to say they'd been offered a council house back on Pits Wood Estate and that she and Bert would arrange for me to return to live with them there. Goodness knows why they wanted to go back there, but I suppose they had friends and it was a familiar place for them.

I didn't hear from them for some months after that and I hoped they might have forgotten about me. I couldn't bare the thought of returning to the estate.

Really, I wanted to stay on the farm, although by that time Helen and Gerald were looking for new jobs and a new house, so I knew things would have to change.

Eventually I received word from Mum, saying they'd settled into this two bedroomed council house and that they'd send the money for me to take the coach back to London. They told me I'd be sharing a bedroom with Iris and of course that made the prospect even worse.

I remember I went around the farm for days in a black mood, telling Helen over and over that I didn't want to go home.

I knew that Gerald had been applying for jobs and just after that Gerald and Helen went away for a week and when they returned they announced that he had secured a job with the Milk Marketing Board as an inspector and that they'd found a small place they wanted to buy near Saltdean in Sussex with some land where they could keep a few goats and start a small dairy business for Helen to manage.

It was quite soon after that, I received the money from Mum for my coach trip and my fate was sealed.

'So how did it come about that you went to live at Saltdean?' Mrs Dyer asks me.

'Helen used to write to me often while I was in London. I think they missed me as much as I did them. Then a little while after they moved down to Saltdean, Helen wrote to my Mum asking if I'd like to go down during the Easter holidays, which of course I did and Mum agreed. Helen came up to London to meet me at Orpington station, where she had a chance to meet Mum.

I had a fantastic time with Gerald and Helen, staying with them for the whole holiday. It was so good to be by the sea again. They had bought three goats by then so I was in my element, feeling as if I was on a mini farm. Helen was beginning to get to grips with learning how to make the cheese and I managed to help her do the milking. My eleven year old hands were better equipped for the task by then.

We went out often, walking the cliff paths and exploring the beaches, although it was still too cold to swim. I hated the thought of returning to London at the end of the holiday and begged Helen and Gerald to let me stay.

I had to go back, of course, to start the next school term, my last one in primary school.

Helen said she'd accompany me all the way home because she wanted to talk to Mum.

Somehow, over a pot of tea in the kitchen, she managed to persuade Mum to let me go and live with them during the summer holiday, before the first term of secondary school started in September. I think it was the promise of finding me a good secondary school there, which may have clinched it. The school I would otherwise attend did not have a very good reputation. Hardly any students ever went on to college or university.'

'And your Mum actually agreed to it?'

I can see Mrs Dyer is not impressed with Mum relinquishing her son so easily.

'To be fair to Mum, I must have been a horrible son during those months. I hated being back on the estate. I still saw some of the old classmates but many had left, including Jimmy whose family had moved to West London. I resented having to keep an eye on my sister all the time as if I was an unpaid child minder. I couldn't get on with Bert and I think I was sullen and unco-operative.

My Mum worked evenings as a cleaner in a school so that Bert would be home to mind Iris, even though Mum didn't leave until it was her bedtime so he didn't really have anything to do. The crunch came one day when I was told to put her to bed while Mum left for work.

Iris could be an angel with Mum, but she was the absolute devil with me. She jumped up and down on the bed, making a scene, calling me names. When I told her off and tried to make her go to bed, she hollered and bawled. Bert, who was sitting with his feet up in the sitting room watching the wrestling, started shouting up the stairs. 'For Chrissake, shut that bloody noise, or similar words to that, 'scuse my language, ladies!

It just made things worse and eventually I slammed out the house and went to sit in the garden shed for an hour.'

'You've never told me that, Jack.' Mavis remarks.

'Not my finest moment, Honey! Anyway, I think that sealed it in Mum's eyes because I was a real pain.

By the end of that very acrimonious term I was packed off to Saltdean and I think she was relieved to see me go. Iris certainly was. I remember the smirk on her face when I left!'

'Do you see your Mum?' Elsie asks.

'Usually once or twice a year I go and see them. Mavis came with me for the day this year. We rub along alright but there's no real warmth there. Iris married last year and lives quite near Mum. They are still close.'

'I'm pleased for Helen and Gerald that you went to live with them, they always treated you like their child.'

'They gave me a good life with them and I see them often. They are my real family now and I'm incredibly grateful to them. They've made quite a little business out of the dairy, breeding more goats, selling the cheeses, yoghurt, milk and butter to delicatessens and the like and Gerald gave up his job to help manage it because it has grown so successful. Helen has a helper in for the heavier manual work.'

'Did you know they bought all my dairy equipment?' Elsie asks. 'I spent time with Helen before they left, making a batch of cheese with her and teaching her the rudiments of dairying, so I hope it helped her get a head start with her goats.'

Mrs Dyer stands up.

'Now, let me show you both around.' She leads us round to her nursery area where she has a range of trees from seedlings right through to large specimens. Many fruit trees and some ornamental flowering, or ones attractive for their foliage or berries.

'Most of the business is commercial but I do get some locals looking for fruit trees or ornamentals for their gardens.'

Mavis asks her if she's got a buyer yet.

'No. I've had some valuations done and I'm just trying to decide which agent to go with. They're all sharks, I just need to decide which one's going to fleece me the least!'

We chat some more about the business and life in general as we stroll amongst the trees.

'Mrs Dyer?'

'Oh, please Jack, and Mavis, call me Elsie. It's far less formal.'

'Elsie, then, did your husband ever come back from the war?'

She pauses for quite a while before answering me.

'He never was at war, Jack. We didn't tell you the truth.'

I must look fairly surprised, although by the time I was ten and

there had been no sign of him, I thought he must have died.
'He was in prison, Jack.'
Now I must look even more surprised. I wasn't expecting that.
'Oh, I didn't realise. Why was he in prison?'
She tells us about his traitorous exploits in the war.
'None of us knew exactly what the Ventnor masts were for then. Now we know they were Radar masts, able to detect German aircraft long before they reached our shores, giving our boys the advantage to intercept them. They were part of Chain Home, a series of similar masts dotted all round the country. They were vital for our security, and there was my traitorous husband selling secrets about them to the Germans. I never even had a clue.'
'Wow. Where is he now?' I ask.
'He's dead now. Died of lung cancer about five years ago. He wanted me to sell the farm when he was inside, but I held out until after the war to get a decent price. I sold up in 1946 and managed to extract enough capital to buy this place.
Arthur had a fifteen year sentence but he was released in 1953. A friend helped him to get a job somewhere not far from Portsmouth as a dairyman. I only saw him once and that was once too many.'
We start to wander back to the garden to collect our jackets.
'Mrs Dyer.., sorry, I mean Elsie', Mavis corrects herself, 'how much will you put the nursery on the market for, if you don't mind me asking?'
I raise my eyebrows at Mavis in surprise. Surely she wasn't thinking it would suit us. We didn't have that sort of money. Elsie looks surprised too, but she tells us the sum she had in mind.
'Out of our league, I'm afraid,' I say, in case Elsie thinks we are prospective buyers.

We take our leave and promise to be in touch again soon.
We stroll hand in hand back to Ventnor in the late afternoon.
Mavis seems thoughtful.
'You're quiet, Honey,' I say.

'I was just thinking about Mrs Dyer. She's quite unique but I like her. Quite blunt! She has a nice place there and she's lucky to live on the Island. It's lovely here.'

We walk along in silence but I can tell Mavis is mulling something else in her mind.

'Jack, when my grandfather died a couple of years ago, he left Dad a sum of money. Dad promised me that when I was in a position to buy a house, that he would give me half of Grandfather's inheritance towards a deposit on it.'

This is all news to me, but Mavis continues.

'It's not a fortune, Jack, but the prices here are much less than prices in Lewes.'

She looks at me for my reaction, but I don't know what to say.

'You look lost for words, Jack!' She gives my hand a squeeze. 'I know quite a lot about trees. I could run that place of Elsie's.'

I laugh. 'Goodness, Mavis, you're a dark horse! I haven't applied for the job yet.'

'I knew you wanted to, though. I saw the advertisement in the paper while it was on the lounge table. And I guessed you'd written to Elsie as well because I heard you asking Helen for the address!'

She gives me a smug look.

'When you sprung this holiday on us I had a pretty good idea what you were up to.'

I'm not as clever as I think I am, and I certainly have a wife who is no fool!

AUTHOR'S NOTES

This is purely a work of fiction although the towns and villages exist on the Isle of Wight.

The farms and characters are all from my imagination.

The six radar masts were in operation during the war, part of Chain Home, and were bombed twice during August 1940. Remnants of three masts can still be seen high on Boniface down.

The Royal Chest Hospital, mainly for tuberculosis patients, was in operation from 1869 to 1964. It was demolished in 1969 and is now the Ventnor Botanic Gardens.

The Isle of Wight took many such evacuees like Jack, some of whom stayed the whole duration of the war.

Front cover painting: by author

ABOUT THE AUTHOR

Kate Bolton

Kate has lived on the Isle of Wight since 1997, with her husband, Keith.
After retiring from teaching and art, she now lives at Niton on the beautiful south coast of the island and spends time writing, painting, gardening and walking.

BOOKS BY THIS AUTHOR

A Marginal Life

The Sound Of Cicadas

A Portrait In Blue

Evacuee

Printed in Great Britain
by Amazon

79823669R00122